ANGEL K

All The
Little
Voices

Copyright © 2023 by Angel Krause

All rights reserved.

No part of this publication may be reproduced, distributed, or transmitted in any form or by any means, including photocopying, recording, or other electronic or mechanical methods, without the prior written permission of the publisher, except as permitted by U.S. copyright law.

The story, all names, characters, and incidents portrayed in this production are fictitious. No identification with actual persons (living or deceased), places, buildings, and products is intended or should be inferred.

Book Cover by Grim Poppy Designs

Interior Formatting by Cat Voleur

Everyone's writing journey looks different and mine started out writing forum based roleplays online. I met a lot of people in my time online, but the one person I will never forget was my dear friend Donna Chavez.

Donna passed away earlier this year and I still haven't found the strength to accept this. She was a dear friend and treasured writing partner. This book, these stories, and my courage to put this out is dedicated to her. To her compassion, to her story, to her kindness, to her strength. We love you so much Donna. You're missed every day.

CONTENTS

The Mirror State	1
There is a Motion at Your Front Door	7
Soul Eater	13
In the Walls	23
A Warning Dismissed	37
A Little Mad	46
There is Only Us	52
Alone	64
A Change in You	98
The Eternal Justice of Man	114
Additional Credits	126

THE MIRROR STATE

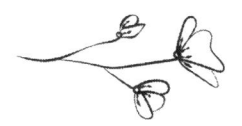

"I don't know why I have to keep going over this." Kim's voice cracked as she shakily held her cigarette up to her lips. "This isn't going to make me comfortable. This didn't start until we moved *here*." Her tone boomed in the otherwise quiet space.

Her partner, Hallie, sighed and shook her head. "Because this has to be about something else. This isn't real, K. These things you're dreaming about. They aren't real. You have to stay grounded in that reality."

There was a grumble and a roll of Kim's eyes. She didn't necessarily think Hallie was wrong. It was more that she hated feeling like a child. It wasn't real? Aggressively putting her cigarette out, she leaned against the wall of their small patio and folded her arms. Even though she was feeling antsy, she did her best to work out the thoughts in her head.

"Okay. Fine." The words came out rushed and irritated. Hallie only gave her a reassuring smile, knowing her partner all too well in regard to sensitive subjects. "It starts with me waking up. I'm on my side of the bed and I'm sitting up to go to the bathroom."

Hallie nodded, sipping her coffee, but remained silent as she paid attention.

"There's this thick, black, standing mirror off to the side. Which, obviously, we don't own a mirror like that. But it's there anyway. As I'm passing it, I can see someone standing behind me, near the entrance to our bedroom. I know it, in the dream. But my dream self won't look. Or hesitate." Kim could feel the pressure in her throat, so she cleared it. "When I come back to get back in bed, I stop and finally notice her. Her hair is black and over her face. She looks wet, but I also can tell she isn't. Her skin is stark white, and her fingers seem to end abruptly, as if they had been removed."

There was a pause. Hallie watched with concern as Kim slid into a sitting position on the concrete slab. Tilting her head, Kim could feel her heartbeat accelerating. She couldn't really explain why this was so difficult to talk about, why the dream had her so bothered. Maybe because it was recurring, or felt so real. Hallie had woken her up screaming more than once because of this dream. Why was it happening? Was Hallie right to believe it was some sort of symbolic manifestation in her mind? Did it mean something, or nothing at all? Kim was frustrated. She had lost sleep and peace of mind.

"Go on, when you're ready," Hallie encouraged with a soft voice.

Finally inhaling to start again, Kim could still picture the dream quite vividly. As though it had happened. As though she just saw this very chain of events. "When I stop to look, I can't get a clear focus before her arms are reaching out and wrapping around my throat." That part was the most difficult. That little piece of the puzzle always made Kim uncomfortable. "I'm reaching for you. I'm calling out to you with a strained voice. And you don't move. You don't wake up. You're not even there." Kim's eyes averted, looking to the ground as she tried to stop herself from getting too emotional.

Hallie leaned forward with her elbows on her knees. "Do you remember if you actually die?" Her fascination with the subject really got under Kim's skin.

"I think I always wake up. I assume I do? But I don't actually know," she replied, standing up and dusting off her jeans. "I'm going to go lie down. Just in case tonight is another restless night." Hallie didn't argue as Kim left the porch and went inside to climb back into bed. Her dreams were the kind she did not remember, which she preferred to the kind she did remember lately.

By the time Kim woke up, she was groggy from sleeping too long. There were no lights on around her, and the windows revealed it was nighttime. "Shit..." she groaned, wondering why Hallie didn't wake her up. "Hallie?" she called out into the dark. There was no answer. Rubbing her eyes, she quickly glanced to the side of the bed, making sure that damn mirror wasn't there. She always had to make sure the girl in the mirror wasn't waiting for her to walk by. The very thought sent a chill down her spine.

The floor creaked slightly as she stepped out into the hallway. It too was dark. There was a faint glow from the stairs. Hallie must have been watching television downstairs or something. It was enough to make Kim move forward. Taking the stairs carefully, as she was still not fully awake, she found her way to the living room. "Hallie?"

Hallie turned to face her with a look that Kim could only find unsettling. "Don't be mad," she said, naturally putting Kim further on edge.

"That's never a good thing." Kim furrowed her brows as Hallie pointed behind her.

"I know this is a big deal, but I want to help. So, I did what I thought would, well, help." Her words lacked confidence and didn't help Kim relax.

Hallie walked around Kim, who followed her with her eyes. In the middle of the foyer was a tall sheet-covered object, and instantly Kim was filled with dread.

"Hallie—" but before Kim could say anything else, Hallie pulled the sheet. Underneath, was a thick, black, standing mirror. The top design curled and tucked in an intricate design, and the corners were slightly cracked from wear and tear. It wasn't new by any means; but it was familiar. Kim was certain she was going to throw up.

"Why?" The word barely left her lips before she found herself walking backwards on autopilot. She wanted to be as far away from the thing as possible.

"I found it in the basement about a week ago. I think this will help. Maybe you saw it when we moved in and just never remembered it? So, it stuck in your head? You must reacquaint yourself with this as just an object. Nothing more. Not a portal. Not a nightmare. Just an object that has no meaning. I know, I should have asked first. But you've been struggling with this for almost two months now, and it's started impacting everyday life. Not just your sleep sometimes." Hallie's voice was full of concern for Kim, but Kim was angry.

It was too real. No longer could she rationalize that this mirror and the girl within it, were not real. A made-up story in her mind. She could touch the mirror. See it. It was right before her eyes. How the fuck was this supposed to help? "You don't understand." Kim answered finally, her eyes threatening to spill over with the emotions she kept locked inside her chest. Going out to the garage, she grabbed a hammer off the small workbench. Twirling it in her hand, she rushed the mirror and raised the hammer.

As the hammer met the glass, it shattered instantly. The noise was much louder than Kim anticipated, and it caused a shriek of surprise to come from Hallie. The corner cracked further and popped off, like a door. Frozen, with the hammer dangling at her side, Kim watched the glass settle on the floor. With her free hand, she reached out, and pried open the wood that had splintered. It was, in fact, a door. Opening it slightly, it revealed a thin stack of shelves for storage. Under normal circumstances, she would have found this intriguing. Instead, she found it only added to her discomfort.

"What is that?" Hallie asked. She had moved a few paces behind Kim after the mirror shattered.

"I don't know. Storage shelves I guess." It was dark on the inside, simply because of the black paint, but there were marks. They almost looked like scratches. "Give me your phone."

Hallie handed over her device without much hesitation. Turning on the flashlight, Kim held the beam over the scratch marks. Etched in horrid, straight lines was the name LYDIA.

Her nerves getting the better of her, she glanced over at Hallie as she dropped the phone onto the floor. "Kim... what is it?"

Shaking her head, she backed away from the mirror. "This isn't real. This isn't real." Her stomach was in knots as her body somehow managed to carry her to a counter in the kitchen, where she sat down. The tears of her dread slid slowly down her cheeks.

"What is going on?" Hallie's voice was suddenly surpassing concern and entering frustration.

"I didn't tell you before. This piece of the dream. It never mattered, because I didn't think it was important, given everything else." Exasperated words left in a mess of spit as she did her best to calm her thoughts.

"Just tell me what it is." Kim shot her head up to look at Hallie, the fear stretched clear across her features.

"Sometimes, when the dream takes longer, I can see her writing her name with her fingers that aren't there. She always writes it in bloody smears that squeak when she starts. It always says 'Lydia' on the other side of the glass."

Hallie didn't look relieved or confused. She turned her head to look at the mirror and a silent gasp fell from her lips. Tilting her head back to look, Kim saw the mirror in the foyer. No more broken glass. Just a perfect reflection. She wanted to call out in surprise. To tell Hallie to run and get out of the house. If she could have made her legs move, she'd have taken it outside to burn it. Instead, she was fixated. Not on the repaired mirror that she had completely ruined only moments before. This time, her eyes were fixated on the reflection itself. It showed the figure next to her was no longer her lover.. Hallie's face had been plastered over in thick, black hair. It looked wet, but she knew it wasn't. Her tan skin was now stark white against the contrast of their yellow lighting. Her fingers looked as though they were missing.

Everything in Kim told her not to look up. Told her to run. To get out. She struggled to even turn her head, unable to catch her breath. Those hands were reaching for her. Extended limbs connected to her throat, knocking her off the counter as she tried to twist away. Before she could get up, she felt the weight of another body atop her, and there was dark hair in her face, obstructing her vision. She couldn't see anything. The nubs of fingers with their missing digits dug into her neck, but as she went to pry them away, she realized the digits weren't missing. They were shredded, meaty remains. She could feel pieces of the bones on certain fingers and just a slimy mess of blood and decay on the others. Something had done this to her. Like she'd had to defend herself. No, like she had an accident. No. Like she had dug herself from her own grave.

THERE IS A MOTION AT YOUR FRONT DOOR

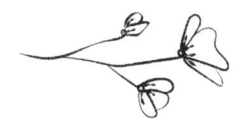

IT WAS NEVER EASY being home alone. I pretty much made sure I always had someone around. Most of my adult life it had been a roommate. Then a husband. Unfortunately, he had to head out of town for a few days for work, and I was left alone. An empty house in a quiet neighborhood. At least when we lived in our apartment, I was still surrounded by people. Something about that notion had always made things less eerie. Less worrisome. Especially these days, where it turns dark before seven at night.

An alert went off on my phone. The email told me a package I had been waiting on was finally delivered. I was eager to see that everything arrived safely, and quickly slid on some sandals to walk to the mailbox. I found myself hesitating when I reached for the knob. All of my lights were on inside and I could tell through the window how dark it already was outside. "It's just outside to get a package." I had done a good enough job of convincing myself it was safe, that I went outside in the dark. To the mailbox. Alone.

Immediately, my phone alerted me: **THERE IS MOTION AT YOUR FRONT DOOR.** It was just me setting off the motion detector. Of course, it also went off for bugs and other 'nothing' things such as that. Avoiding looking around, I knew I'd find something unsettling. Something always felt off being outside at night. I mean, how many movies or shows have you seen when something horrible happens to someone outside at night?

Closing the box, I made it halfway up the drive before I felt the wind pick up. A chill shot through me, and I pulled the package into my chest immediately. Glancing behind me, down the street, I gasped. At the fence line of my neighbor's yard, I was certain I saw something moving on the ground. Crawling maybe? Toward the street? I had to be imagining things. The wind could have easily created shadows from the trees moving. It was just my mind playing tricks on me. It had to be.

Swallowing the fear that was building rather quickly, I all but ran for my front door. My phone notified me there was motion at my front door once more. "Just me, you silly thing." Thankfully, it only took a few minutes for the worry to fall away. Inside, in the light, things felt much safer to me. "Now let's see." My words were still quiet in the empty house as I locked the door behind me. I opened my box to make sure everything was intact; you never knew when something was going to take forever, then also be broken.

"Perfect," I said out loud in my dining room, putting my new custom silverware set back in the box and picking up my phone. Just as I turned to move into my living room, there was an alert on my phone **THERE IS MOTION AT YOUR FRONT DOOR.**

My heart raced a bit. Just enough to make me hesitate in my footing. I had not forgotten the slithering mass I saw only moments before. Quick to check the camera, it took a moment for me to see, to notice the black mass sliding up the driveway. It disappeared as it reached the bottom of my steps. It was so hard to judge the size based on the view of the camera.

A dog? A wild animal? I remained frozen. Then, I could hear it. *Thud. Thud. Thud.* Heavy hits fell on each of my stairs, leading directly to my front door. My phone lit up again; **THERE IS MOTION AT YOUR FRONT DOOR.** Shaking fingers unlocked my screen. Entire body locking up, I was certain I was going to throw up. I was terrified. Lifting the phone closer to my face, I selected the notification to view the camera.

Nothing.

I went back.

Nothing.

I went back to the notification before, and nothing.

In shock, I thought maybe I really was getting into my own head. Being alone at night had always been an uneasy thing for me, and surely this could be dismissed as just being on edge. Once more, I glanced at the last notification. I just needed one more view to believe nothing was there. Only this time, something *was* there. The light on my porch flickered on the screen, and in a flash, there was a black outline standing in front of the camera.

I gasped loudly as my free hand flew up to cover my mouth. It looked like a human body. There was nothing else truly distinguishing about it. Snapping its neck and arms, it twitched and pointed towards the camera. I couldn't look away. I was mesmerized. The lights flickered again and as if it had jumped forward, its face was taking up my entire screen. Immediately I stumbled backwards into my couch, causing me to fall over onto the cushions, and drop my phone. A breathy sound came from my phone, while I couldn't seem to blink.

The knob turned ever so slightly. From my current spot on the couch, I didn't see it. I could hear it though. Intentionally drawing out the inevitable. Was this *thing* toying with me? Slowly, the lock slid out of place and the door shoved open so hard it slammed into the coat rack on the other side. I couldn't get my bearings. I tried three times to stand up and look at whatever had just come into my home, but I couldn't get up. So, I waited. *Thud. Thud. Thud.* I could hear the weight shifting on the steps leading up from my foyer. I closed my eyes. Trying to steady my breathing, I just waited.

Nothing.

I waited for what felt like hours.

Nothing.

I jumped and yelped at the sound of the front door slamming shut. Something in the moment gave me the courage to open my eyes. Still, there was nothing to see. Consumed with dread, I stood up finally. Peeking over the top of my stairs,

I saw an empty space. The door was locked. There was no figure. No sign that the door had been open at all. Confused, I stood speechless for several moments. Then, I heard it. That breathing from the camera. Only this time, I no longer had my phone in my hand. The sound was coming from behind me.

Slowly, I turned to see what it was. All the lights flickered at once, just like the light outside had. My eyes landed on the same figure as before. It stood there, motionless, in front of me. Outlines, barely visible. I opened my mouth to scream, and internally I begged my legs to run. Instead, the shape eased farther and farther away. There was a pressure on my chest and my back slammed into the stairs. My movements did not halt until I rolled into the front door. Blinking away my disorientation, everything hurt.

I had to get out of my house. I had to leave and get help. My phone was up there with that *thing*, and I was in no shape to be on the run. So, I tried to crawl. It was all I had control over at that moment. The lights steadily flickered, and the shape was now morphing onto all fours and rushing down the stairs directly toward me. I screamed. I closed my eyes. Whatever was going to happen, I couldn't stop it. There was no saving myself. Not this time.

The breathing stopped suddenly. It was like that feeling you get when you know something is there, but you can't hear it. It was close to my face. Mere inches. I could hear the downstairs door open and slowly a shuffling sound was heard. Was it leaving me alone? Once again, confusion set in. I felt a hand on my arm and snapped it away, screaming and finally opening my eyes.

"What? What's wrong?" My husband stood over me, completely baffled by the state I was in. "Did you fall down the stairs? Should I call the ambulance? Oh my god, are you alright?" I didn't understand. I couldn't explain myself, even if I knew what had happened.

"I... I fell," was all I managed. He helped me stand and my ankle was hurt. Sitting me at the bottom of the stairs, he looked me over.

"Where is your phone?" I pointed upstairs and he left to retrieve it. "Here, let me help you stand." Taking the phone from him, I put my arm around his neck. We didn't get to round the stairs to leave for the garage before my screen lit up.

The sound was all too familiar as I read the notification on my phone. **THERE IS MOTION AT YOUR FRONT DOOR.**

SOUL EATER

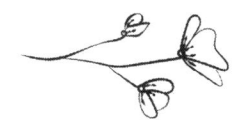

I'll never understand.

That was the first thought that went through Father Cameron Monroe's head as he stared at the Mare family sitting awkwardly at their dining room table. Just the mother and father.

"Wh-whatever it costs, we'll do it! Please... you have to help our daughter."

If I had a nickel, was what Father Monroe thought as he stood before the trembling father and horrified mother. *Their daughter,* Cameron thought, looking to the wooden door that was nailed shut from the outside. He shook his head in contemplation. Could this one be real?

It didn't seem likely, given everything he had seen in his decade as a priest. This felt drastic though, even for Christians. By this point, Cameron had seen and experienced it all. He himself had even been possessed during a routine exorcism. *Routine*. That wasn't really a word meant to be used in such context. From that day forward, Cameron never underestimated God's willingness to let someone suffer. It was the first time he had ever known doubt as a priest.

"Tell me again." Cameron's voice was even, but firm. "What happened before these odd occurrences?" The father nodded, his face showing clear signs of defeat. From the stress lines around his mouth and cheeks, to the dark pillows beneath his worn eyes. There was a time, the priest guessed, when the man's cloudy gaze had once been blue instead of gray. A time, perhaps, when the pain didn't exist.

Cameron wasn't a *true* monster. He hated seeing humans suffer. He hated knowing they worshipped something that didn't give a flying fuck about them. Cameron seethed as he tried to relax and took a seat at the worn wooden table. The father explained that he didn't think his daughter had done anything to invite a spirit in, answering a question that most men in his field would have asked. It had taken a great deal of effort to get Mr. Mare to calm down enough to tell Cameron what was going on in the first place. The initial phone call was saturated with emotion. Understanding the family's plight, it still made it difficult for the priest to get through his questions.

What he did know was that they didn't believe their daughter was into any sort of devil worship. She had gone to the docks with a few friends and when she came back that night it was like the lights in her mind were on, but no one was home. Cameron furrowed his brows. Nothing this man said gave him any inclination as to what could have actually happened. Their daughter could have come back different for any number of reasons. However, when Cameron tried to ask the hard questions, Mr. Mare wasn't having it. "Does your daughter have a boyfriend? Is it possible something else could have—?"

Mr. Mare's hands had flown up as if the motion of doing so could have physically prevented Father Monroe from saying anything further. "Absolutely not. We know our daughter. This is demonic. This is... this is something else!"

Now, sitting with them, Cameron recounted the events and sighed heavily. "Still, the nails? I assume she grew violent?" The mother nodded, but as soon as she opened her mouth she began to sob uncontrollably. Her frail arms lifted ever so slightly, so that her hands could hide her emotions from the near stranger across from her.

"We woke up the other morning, 'round three, and she was sitting on my wife's chest with a knife to her throat." As if on cue, Mrs. Mare's hands dropped to her throat. He hadn't noticed a mark of any kind, and she was clearly still alive.

The father looked down at the ground, his eyes brimming with all the pain he felt for his daughter. *It's too early to tell if this is an act or not.* Cameron sighed. Three. Of course it was three. This mocking of the trinity was proof enough of how childish, and yet predictable, unclean spirits could be. "I've heard enough Mr. Mare. Can you get me a tool to remove the nails? I'm going to go in and meet your daughter." Mr. Mare, or Jacob, as Father Monroe recalled, looked surprised. Waiting for him to move, the priest shifted a bit, "What is her first name?"

Mr. Mare finally snapped out of his hesitating stupor. "Her name is Katie." Nodding, Cameron pulled his rosary from inside his garments and wrapped it around his wrist and his middle finger. Grabbing his book and the small vial of blessed water he brought inside with him, he tried to center his focus.

There was still the very real possibility that he was going into that room to find a broken, neglected child. Over the years of performing these so-called *exorcisms*, he had seen just how depraved *these* people could be. These followers of a greater good. These men and women of justice and love. *What a bunch of bullshit.*

Conveniently, the hammer had been resting on a counter in the kitchen. Items placed in a convenient spot were a sign of a staged event as well. The bitterness of his own history with these people was clouding his judgment. He had to remain unbiased until he obtained proof, one way or the other. Cameron took the hammer from Mr. Mare and carefully approached the door.

When he touched the outside of it, it felt almost hot to the touch. That was something he hadn't expected. He began to pull the large nails from the door, despite the unease settling beneath his skin. Taking a deep breath, he pulled the final nail and the weight of the door shifted. For a moment, Cameron wondered if the door was going to fall over on him. He rolled his shoulders back, and took his first step into the room.

The first thing he noticed was that it was dark and cold. The sort of cold that made your lungs tighten as though there was no oxygen to take in. There was very little to see just yet, but he was surprised how empty the room felt. There was nothing inviting about it, or warm. As he moved into the room, it was as though all the sound had completely vanished. His ears were ringing from the silence. Cameron remained still for just a moment as he existed in the void. *Fuck.* All at once the smell of rot wrapped around his sense of smell like a molded blanket. Dense and suffocating.

Cameron's eyes adjusted to the darkness and in the far right corner of the room, he saw slight movement. Just enough to tell him it was the girl. She faced the corner and her knees appeared to be up in her chest. "Are you here to help me?" She sounded like she had been crying, but her voice shifted at the end of her question. It was as if her throat needed to be cleared. Kids were a hard thing for Cameron. Taking this path with his life, he didn't have any of his own. *How can they worship something that would do this?* A question he often wondered. His jaw grew taut as he thought of the answer so many people gave. 'God's will.' Or, his personal favorite, 'Everything has a reason.' Yes, because it was simple to justify an all mighty being's cruelty by saying 'He did it because He wanted to.'

There was a sour taste in his mouth, but he had to push it aside. It was not the time to do his usual back and forth with himself. "I am. Katie, can you tell me if you're hurt?" He was cautious moving closer.

The lights in the room flickered on and off for a moment, before finally deciding to stay on. Glancing around the small space, he tried to get a lay of the land. The floor, though neat, was littered with dark stains. Not wanting to assume it was anything other than normal kid marks, he turned his attention to the walls. Immediately, he noticed the markings above her headboard. Deeply rooted scratches had all but shredded the faded yellow wallpaper. Her bedding looked as though it had been washed with mud. The conditions were less than desirable and it was hard to shake that this might just be another abuse case.

The sound had not yet returned to the room. Silence remained a moment longer before he heard the fast approaching steps of the girl he had taken his eyes off of for too long. Before he had a chance to react, Katie had launched herself into him, knocking him to the ground. His book dropped to the floor and he dropped the bottle he held.

"Help me! Help me!" the girl called out, slashing towards Cameron's face. It wasn't until her fingers connected to the side of his cheek that he realized she didn't have any nails left. Bloody fingertips smacked against his skin. Cameron tried to stop her, but it was taking him a moment to get his head back in the game.

Peering up at the girl, all that remained before him was her shell. Her eyes were sunken in, and her cheek bones were protruding. Her skin sagged, loosely hanging on by a thread to the skeleton inside her form. The reality hit him then; she looked as though she wasn't going to last much longer. Surprisingly strong for her clearly weakened state, Father Monroe had to fight to regain control of the situation. Grabbing her wrist to keep her fingers away from his face and neck, he tried to control her thrashing. "Katie, if you can hear me, I need you to tell me you're there. Show me you're there." He was raising his voice, but the girl wasn't loud enough for him to need to shout.

Then, all at once, the sound returned. As the noises of their scuffle became quieter somehow, Katie was yelling down at him. Her body was still slightly on top of his as Cameron was pushing her back enough to sit upright. "Listen to me, Katie you have to-" His words were abruptly cut short when her neck violently twitched from side to side for a moment. Her eyes darkened and her mouth fell open, and suddenly he knew where the smell of decay was coming from. "No. No. No."

The girl's voice was getting deeper and deeper. "Time to pay your fee, Father!" As her head fell forward, he watched the girl's hands reach out for his own throat. In a hurry, he rolled with the girl on top of him. He pinned her to the floor with his left hand, while moving the right hand upward. His rosary lowered to the girl's cheek.

"Saint Michael the Archangel, defend us in battle," Cameron began the rite of exorcism. This wasn't what he had hoped, and he now had to focus on the job at hand.

Cameron's first brush with possession was also a young child. The boy's name was Thomas and Thomas' parents were the worst excuse for parents Cameron had ever seen. They had Thomas tied with chains to a post in the middle of an abandoned silo. Their house was a good three miles away and they had left the boy there to rot.

As Father Monroe happened upon Thomas, he was already prepared to call child services. In those days, he truly had never experienced a true demonic take over of a human body. Instead, most were mental illness or total lies. The reason for the lies varied case to case, but generally it was for attention or popularity. *You see enough movies and suddenly you want to be in one.*

Thomas was different. That night, as Cameron managed to cut away the chains, he learned what real evil looked like. Only one person left that silo alive. Thomas had broken Cameron's collarbone, three ribs, his nose, and had managed to cut the Achilles tendon in the priest's right ankle. Thomas' parents seemed relieved their son was dead. There was a lingering moment for Cameron, as he realized that their hatred for their child could have been what opened him up for the devil to play with. A similar notion sat in the back of his mind again; what did the parents do to make Katie so vulnerable to evil? What was her life like before the change? Was her father to blame? Did her mother know?

The girl's body twisted and contorted as she tried to move away from him. The thoughts of Thomas drifted back in the shadows of Father Monroe's mind. "You need a penny. Just a penny will do. Give me a penny. On the boat I'll carry you." The sing-song voice made him uncomfortable, but he had to move forward. He had to keep going. A penny? His mind contemplated what this meant and what demon was tormenting the little girl.

"Be our protection against the wickedness and snares of the devil;

"May God rebuke him, we humbly pray;

"And do thou, O Prince of the Heavenly Host, by the power of God, thrust into hell Satan and all evil spirits who wander through the world for the ruin of souls. Amen."

Lifting his rosary, he performed a Signum Crucis over his chest as he kissed the rosary. Using his mouth, he managed to reach the bottle of holy water and sprinkled it slowly over where the girl's heart would be. "Stay with me, Katie." He spoke only to the human spirit; not the dark one.

"Row, row, row your boat..." she whistled and sang the lyrics off and on. Amusement flashed across her features as Cameron looked down annoyed.

"You will leave this child of God, unclean spirit. Tell me your name. You have no power here!"

The girl let out a roar of laughter. "I will eat your spirit, priest. You will roam the world with me in your bosom and there's *nothing—*" but Cameron didn't let it continue. With his eyes opened and frontward facing, he continued his prayers.

"Come to the assistance of men whom God has created to His likeness and whom He has redeemed at a great price from the tyranny of the devil. The Holy Church venerates you as her guardian and protector; to you, the Lord has entrusted the souls of the redeemed to be led into heaven."

This time, the girl began to convulse, with a thick white foam coming from her mouth. *No. No. No!* Cameron climbed off the girl and put her on her side. The moment he pushed on her cheeks to clear her airway; she was thrown backwards into a side table. The lamp from the surface fell in a loud crash onto the floor, shattering into pieces that were now launching themselves into the air towards Father Monroe.

"You have a darkness in you, priest. You mustn't ignore the call! Knock. Knock. Answer me!" Katie's body stood up, but as she moved forward, her toes dragged across the floor. Three loud banging sounds at the door could be heard. "Let me taste you... Cameron..." The voice was not Katie's, but that of the spirit inside of her. "Just. One. Bite."

With the remainder of his vial, he splashed water at the girl still moving toward him. Watching in disbelief, Cameron witnessed the girl slowly inch into a floating stance right before him. Her legs kicked out, catching him off guard, and he was pushed into the wall on the same side of the room he entered. Katie's face contorted. Her eyes were filled with tears. "I-I'm sorry." There she was. That was her.

With a newfound courage and sense of urgency, Cameron pushed on. "Pray therefore the God of Peace to crush Satan beneath our feet, that he may no longer retain men captive and do injury to the Church. Offer our prayers to the Most High, that without delay they may draw His mercy down upon us; take hold of the dragon, the old serpent, which is the devil and Satan, bind him and cast him into the bottomless pit that he may no longer seduce the nations. Leave this child of God! Leave her now!"

Cameron could feel the tension in the air shift. It was thick on his skin, like sweat to his brow. "You must pay a penance, priest." The last of the words spoken, Katie's mouth opened slowly. At first, the priest thought she was about to speak. It wasn't until it opened unnaturally wide, that he noticed the head of a small black snake slithering forward. It squirmed across her cheek and down the side of her neck. No matter how hard he tried to move, he couldn't. His legs failed him. He remained in the same stance, fixated on the scene before him. He was forced to watch as the snake slid around Katie's arm and dropped to the floor next to where her feet floated off the carpet. In a trance, he watched as the narrow pink tongue slipped between poisonous lips and sped up in his direction.

Trying to fight the hold this creature had on him, he couldn't get away from it. Katie's body remained frozen, only now her eyes were closed and color was starting to return to her cheek. Was this the price? In order to save this child's life, was Cameron to accept this demon as his own? By the time he was able to pull his gaze downward, the snake's head was lifted up so their eyes could meet. It looked much larger now. The snake wasted no time and slowly, and painfully, began forcing its way into his mouth.

Gagging, the priest tilted his head back but couldn't move his arms to dislodge the creature from the opening. No prayer came to mind, and no faith was left on his tongue. Cameron fell forward, grabbing his throat and choking on the leathery form that wiggled into his digestive track. Then all at once, the lump in his throat and his belly was gone. Katie fell somewhere on the floor next to him. The commotion drew in her parents, who rushed to her side.

The gagging ceased and Cameron rolled onto his back. He couldn't catch his breath. His ears were ringing and his eyes felt as though they were on fire. Everything hurt and everything felt sick. Everything felt *wrong*. *The Bible says those who are born again through Christ can never be taken by the enemy.* That was what his teacher had told him. So why did this happen? Why Cameron? His body was supposed to be protected. Why wasn't he worthy of God's protection? Why wasn't this young girl worthy of His protection?

Sitting up, Cameron stifled a grunt. Neither parent paid the priest any mind at first. A slight taste of guilt sat beneath the surface, as he felt bad for assuming the parents might be lying, abusive pricks. Mr. Mare came forth eventually, questioning what happened and whether or not the priest was okay. "I'm fine. G-go get your bible. Have her recite a passage. So long as she is able to do so, you will know the demon is gone." It wasn't the only way to know, but considering that the beast was now in his belly, he knew it would no longer torment young Katie Mare.

Cameron forced himself to his feet, sliding across the floor in a weakened state. The hand with the rosary wrapped around it was burning like a rash. It festered, itchy and irritated. Finding the closest bathroom, Cameron took to the sink. Removing his rosary, there was a deep red outline from where the beading had been. Fear was an afterthought. He was consumed by exhaustion and hunger. He did, however, recognize rage and disappointment. He felt empty. Rinsing off his face, he glanced at his reflection; only it wasn't his familiar face that looked back. It was the face of a monster.

Around his head, Cameron could see a tattered, worn cloak. It was a dark brown material and for a moment he thought he could almost feel it move against his cheeks. The face inside the hood was a skeletal one. Teeth missing from his broken smile, but not all his flesh had decayed away. Instead, fragmented pieces of old muscle and tissue remained. Around his nose and parts of his eye sockets, it clung to bone. His eyes were sunken in but painted over with a deep crimson watercolor.

Something that didn't add up at first, until Cameron remembered the song. It played on repeat in his head now. "Row, row, row your boat..." the words coming from his own lips, while the face without a mouth simply appeared to grin at him. Charon, the ferryman. The collector of souls to the underworld. He simply smiled and gave Cameron a wink, nestling beneath his skin as the priest gripped the sink and watched the last shred of his humanity fade into nothing. There were no answers here today, only more questions. The most important being, why was

Charon, an ancient psychopomp from another mythos, taking over the body of an eight-year-old little girl?

In the Walls

Introductions

Taryn pulled up in the driveway, and for the first time in years the house moved. She watched Taryn size her up, glancing over the broken and dirty exterior. There was a desire within her walls to reach out to help Taryn as she stepped over the cracked walk up and the overgrown garden. The house watched her carefully. A hopeful glance, balancing itself with concern. Would she stay? Would she abandon it, like all those before her?

Taryn approached the door and picked up the lock box on the outside. Checking her phone, there was a code the realtor had sent her that she would use to get inside. The lock turned and the box beeped, but when she turned the knob she couldn't get it to budge. Not wanting to cause any damage to the entrance, she stepped back and looked up at the towering mess of a building. Something about it was calling to her. She had to get inside.

The house watched her as she tried the windows she could reach. Nothing budged, but she heard a rattling from the front that caught her attention. Wondering if the agent had changed her mind about meeting her, she peered around the empty driveway. Trudging through the tall grass, she noticed the garage door was opened a little more than it had been.

"Odd," Taryn said aloud, looking around as if to pacify a curiosity regarding who could have opened it.

Stepping over what appeared to be broken glass and metal pieces, she ducked low enough to manage to get into the garage. Pulling her phone from her back pocket, she turned on the flashlight. The garage was full of stuff. Most of it was wrapped in tarps or stacked in boxes. Taryn couldn't find the door for a moment, because it was hidden behind some sort of tall cabinetry system.

Leaning against the side of it, she pushed as hard she could. The echo of fake wood sliding across concrete filled the air. Taryn winced at the sound, but didn't stop until it cleared the path to the door. Three brick steps led up to the door. Placing her foot on the first step, a piece of the brick was loose and tripped her up as she collided into the door. It sprang open with very little effort and Taryn almost face-planted into the floor.

Grunting as she got her footing again, she grumbled and dusted herself off. "Brilliant." Her frustration built, but she had to admit this was such a unique renting opportunity.

The room Taryn found herself in was a kitchen. It was pretty basic, and surprisingly empty given the state of the garage. Flipping a switch, the room became only slightly better lit. *How can air look yellow?* Taryn thought to herself. Everything was covered in dust. Pieces of the vinyl flooring were curling up. There were dents and holes on some of the walls. The fridge door sat crooked and Taryn scrunched her nose, certain the putrid smell was coming from inside.

There were missing cabinet doors. The stove was crooked. The faucet was completely removed, and sat rusted on the top of the counter next to the sink. "Welp..." huffing for a moment, Taryn put her hands on her hips and moved into the front of the house.

She moved thoughtfully from the kitchen, into a small dining room, then to the living room. Everything was empty, and sad. There was no brightness to anything she laid eyes on. The furnishings were broken, dingy, and messy. This was going to take a lot to get going and be ready for someone to move in.

"I'll figure it out," Taryn said out loud. "There's something about you..."

The house suddenly grew a bit brighter. Darkness vanished from the corners of the room as she went down the short hall to the two bedrooms. There was more dust, and more broken parts. The guest bedroom closet was missing a door altogether and the master closet doors were off their tracks. A small laugh escaped Taryn as she spun around.

Pulling out her phone, she dialed the agent she was working with and waited four rings for an answer.

"I completely understand if it isn't for you..." the agent started.

A scoff of disbelief escaped Taryn's mouth, "Are you kidding? She's perfect. I did want to ask..." there was a slight pause as Taryn noticed the master bedroom becoming even brighter. "Do you think I could get a lower rent if I agreed to fix the place up?"

The quiet on the other line caused Taryn concern that maybe the agent couldn't hear her. Just as she was about to repeat herself, the agent returned with a tone of confusion. "You want to live there?"

Another laugh escaped Taryn. "Uh, yeah? Aren't you supposed to be selling me on it? It really is perfect. I can get this place all cleaned up. She just needs some love and effort."

The rest of the conversation was about moving in details. All the while, the house grew warm on the inside. The bowels of the home came to life and there was finally a vibration within her veins. The agent couldn't lower the monthly price, but she agreed to waive the deposit and cut the first month's rent in half. More than a deal, Taryn told her she'd send over the files when she got them signed that night.

Exiting the way she came, Taryn yanked down on the garage door to close it all the way. Standing back with her hands on her hips, she smiled. "See you soon." Blowing it a kiss, she turned to walk and stumbled on the broken driveway. Her knees slammed down onto the concrete, a rock cutting into her skin and causing a thick line of blood to spill over and down her chin onto the concrete.

"Fuck!" she exclaimed, watching the blood seep into her sock and still collecting around her shoe. "Great..."

There was far more blood than there was pain. Going over to her car, she opened the driver side and climbed in to find a napkin. A few moments later, Taryn pulled out of the driveway, smiling at the house that she was unaware was smiling back.

Moving Day

The moving truck backed into the driveway as Taryn motioned for them to keep going. Holding her hands up, she mouthed a 'whoa' and the truck came to a halt. "Perfect!" she yelled out, with a thumbs up.

It had taken her almost a week to finish arranging things to the point she could move in. Glancing at her new place, she felt energetic and optimistic about the next stage of her life. Her brother, Joe, jumped out of the moving truck and sighed.

"You gotta lotta work ahead of ya, T." He eyed over the overgrown nature of the front of the house.

"Consider it bonding time with my new place. Also, just let me be happy maybe?" Taryn rolled her eyes, opening the envelope with her new keys and going to the front door. The house was unamused by the body shame that was placed upon her. Who did this human think he was?

The lockbox had been completely removed and surprisingly with the key turned in, the door opened easily. Grateful it didn't stick like last time, she presumed it had something to do with the lockbox and not the actual door itself.

Walking inside, she could hardly believe what she saw. The living room that once had holes in the walls, was patched up. A slightly wet looking spot was caked over the places she distinctly remembered having missing paint or holes all the way through. *Huh, they must have done some clean-up...*

"Damn," she said aloud, earning a quizzical brow from her brother. "They must have cleaned up the place after I left. There's no more holes. The faucets are corrected and the closet door seems to be back on the track."

Joe didn't pay much mind, but was always busying himself outside with boxes. "I got a long drive home tonight after I drop this thing off, let's get this done." The house creaked in annoyance.

"Yeah," Taryn said, tracing her fingers over the wall leading to the front. "You're beautiful," she whispered. A few drops of water fell from the sink as the house felt the words Taryn said. No one had called her beautiful before.

Joe and Taryn's relationship was a bit strained because of their childhood. Joe was still the loving son and Taryn was the child that got out into the real world and realized her parents sucked. She had been surprised when she reached out and he agreed to help her to begin with. They hadn't talked in a couple of years after a bad argument at her parents' attempted Christmas dinner.

Without much more dallying, Taryn went outside to start pulling stuff out of the truck. She didn't have a lot. Her bed, a sofa, a dresser, a couple of small tables, and a banged up desk. It took them only a couple of hours to empty the truck and get furniture sorted where it was going to go. Taryn made a mental note to see what else she might find in the garage.

The day had her feeling full of what she could only describe as joy. It wasn't exactly a feeling Taryn was used to. "Do you wanna order in a pizza and watch a movie?"

Silence lingered as Joe processed what she was asking, and Taryn's heart pounded in her ears. She could feel her face grow hot as her fear of rejection turned into reality. "I have to go, T. Glad you got everything in. We'll uh, we'll catch up soon."

The look on his face as he backed away and walked out of the front door made Taryn sick to her stomach. How could she have even expected a different outcome? She had spent her entire life alone. Having a sibling wasn't supposed to feel that way. It wasn't supposed to hurt all the time. The door closed loudly, probably more from her feelings than the actual sound it made.

As Taryn looked around, the silence was overwhelming. Two tears slid down her cheeks as she scratched her nails into her palms. It was getting late, but she knew she wasn't going to be going to bed anytime soon. So instead, she worked. She focused on boxes and getting things settled. Starting with the kitchen, she cleaned out the cabinets to prep them for her dishes. She wiped off counters to prepare them for her smaller appliances and a few decorative items.

It is just you and me now. The thought wasn't one she heard, but one she felt. She nodded in agreement. "Just you and me." She said aloud to the house.

<u>The Slipup</u>

The first week in the house had been going really well. Taryn was completely finished moving in and things were finally starting to feel like home. She made note of certain things just to make sure she didn't get blamed for them. There was a crack in the wall near the front door, and a few dents in the flooring leading into the bedroom. She also found some separation around the window frames and the wall. The house itself was clearly dated, but she knew it was mostly just neglected.

Oh, how she had been so neglected. Taryn brought happiness into every room with her and the house reveled in it.

She had already spoken to the company about some of the repairs, and they agreed to send someone to help with the things Taryn wouldn't be able to fix herself. She had set an alarm to make sure she was up for their arrival, but of course they were late. It was just like anything else. Even if they gave you a window, they were coming after that window. That had always been her experience.

There was an aggressive knock on the front door causing Taryn to spill her coffee cup when she jumped from the sudden noise. The house radiated annoyance, and so did Taryn.

Opening the door, she peered out at the brutish man who stood there. His face was thick and overly tanned. His hair was pulled back out of his face, he had a bucket at his feet with items, and his arms were crossed high on his broad chest.

"Morning," Taryn said, more than clearly agitated.

"Well, morning. Here to fix some cracks?" He eyed Taryn up and down, and immediately she thought she was going to vomit.

Trying to reassure herself that the company she was renting from wouldn't have sent this oaf if they hadn't used him before, she still didn't really want him in her home. The house agreed as the door slammed accidentally behind him as he entered.

Her eyes went to the door, confused. She figured if the air was on or there was a breeze, this might not be uncommon. Motioning for the strange male to follow her, she led him to her bedroom where the cracks were around the window.

"Your room, huh?" Taryn ignored his comment and stepped back towards the door.

"There's always some dents in the flooring here, I mostly just want to make sure I'm not at risk of falling through the boards. And then there's another crack along the wall near the front door."

He eyed her for a moment before he looked at the window and grunted. Stepping around her, she had to hurry to move for fear of him knocking her over. He was quite a bit larger than her. The sense of unease growing in her belly, she watched him bounce on the flooring and push around the dents.

"I'm guessing just warped. Let me work on the front door first and we'll see."

Thankful he was going to start working, she went back to her computer. She had taken some time off from her remote job to get settled. Taryn picked up random data entry jobs to provide her income. It was enough, usually, and had been a big reason she couldn't afford much for a place to live.

The house really enjoyed this time of day with Taryn. It was normally just the two of them and it rather preferred the peace and harmony that came during those few hours a day it was like this.

It must have been an hour or so before the man approached her again. "The front door is going to be a foundation issue I think. I can patch it, but when the weather changes again or if it rains, you'll notice more showing up sooner or later."

Taryn and the house sighed, the air coming on to reflect the house's feelings. That was not what either wanted to hear. "Okay, thanks."

The guy lingered in the kitchen looking at her and she shifted in the chair. "Was there something else?" She finally asked.

"Nope." He continued to stand and stare.

Narrowing her eyes, the unease shifted to anger. "Please finish what you're here to do. I have work to do." Her tone was even, but stern.

The guy scoffed and called her a 'bitch' under his breath, before heading back to his work. After a few moments of contemplating what to do, she heard screaming coming from her bedroom. Scrambling to get up, she followed the sound. How does it sound so far away when it's so close?

Taryn ran towards her room and was frozen in the doorway by what she was seeing. The repair man was hanging in the air and the left side of his body was attached to the wall in a way Taryn could only describe as melted. Blood gushed down the floor and to the carpet. He was calling out in agony and she could hear his bones crushing, somehow louder than his screams.

Falling to her rear on the floor, she balled up, closed her eyes, and covered her ears with her hands. It felt like hours before the screaming finally stopped. Taryn opened her eyes and gasped, wishing she hadn't. The wall had cracked further, and it appeared to be chewing on the second half of the man's body.

The amazing part wasn't just the gore and now presumably dead body, but the way the house moved to consume him without causing damage to the rest of the room. How is this even possible?? The wall barely vibrated from the action. It was able to take in so much, it was hard to believe that the only thing that came out onto the floor was blood. There were no body parts, no skin or tissue, nothing but dark red ichor.

Taryn let her hand wander out to her side to grab the doorframe. Using it to pull herself up, she couldn't take her eyes away from the window. Only a few more motions and the body was gone. Other than the red sludge dripping down the wall and creating a large puddle on the floor, there was no other evidence the man was even there.

Everything went still and silent. Fumbling back, Taryn stepped into the hallway. Her foot sunk slightly into a dip and then just as quickly was flat again. The dents filled themselves. The crack around her window was completely fixed. Another shuffling sound was heard from towards the front. Although she was sure she knew what was happening, she went to see the front door for herself.

It was perfect. It didn't stop there. Taryn looked around and noticed more chipped paint looked brand new. The rusted over handles on the door to the pantry behind her looked replaced. The tinge of yellow on the ceiling was completely erased. It was like the house was healing itself. As though that human happy meal had made it feel better? *Her.* It made her feel better.

Perhaps even weirder than that, was how good Taryn felt. She felt energized and happy. It was like a fog had been lifted from her brain, and her body felt rejuvenated. Shifting the weight between her two feet, it was getting difficult to stand still.

Sit. She heard, and didn't bother arguing. Finding her way to the edge of the couch, she sat in contemplation. *What am I going to do?* She had just watched her house eat a human being. Now she was realizing those things she had been feeling and hearing had a source. The source was the house. It was all around her.

Taryn sat, trying to keep her breathing under control. There had been an immediate connection to this place. She just knew. Something was different about this house, even from before. *Did the agent know this? Is that why she wouldn't come inside? Is that why she was so eager to just get someone in?* Her mind was racing with questions.

It didn't take Taryn long to remember the differences when she came in on moving day. Things were better, but they had only changed after she bled in the driveway.

Looking around the walls and ceilings she asked out loud, "Is that what keeps you going? Blood?"

There was nothing at first. Taryn felt frustrated and immediately laughed, thinking she had completely lost her mind. Then, the hairs on her neck stood up and she felt something around her. A quiet, invisible voice whispered to her, **Yes.**

Jumping, Taryn stood in the center of the living room and shook her head. This was insane. "Well how the hell do we get rid of the van? They're going to know something happened to him!" She was yelling at a house. An inanimate object.

Fear was creeping into her thoughts. She'd never find something like this for this price. She couldn't afford to move again. Her brother coming to help was a huge favor and she knew there was no asking him a second time. *What the fuck am I going to do?*

Shh. She heard the house attempting to soothe her worries. Taryn knew there was no way she could live with this knowledge. They'd never believe a house killed this man and she'd be held responsible. What was even the deal? Would she have to bring people for the house to murder? That's what this was. The guy was a sleaze but that didn't mean he deserved to be eaten alive.

"And what about me? Am I even safe here?"

Safe. Yes.

She didn't understand it, but she heard these things so clearly, as though she was standing right next to a person that had said them. It wasn't the most unsettling part, but it still mattered. It certainly added to the chaos of the situation.

Rushing into her room, Taryn threw a duffle on her bed and threw in things as quickly as she could. She'd go sleep in her car for a night if she had to. She needed to get away from this house. To give herself space, and to come up with a plan. As she reached the door, she hesitated. "I'm sorry." She whispered.

The inside of the home grew cold, and water began to drip from every faucet. Air conditioning grew louder as each step away from her that Taryn took, the house was in pain. Agony. Feeling of grief and loss consumed her. No one could ever love her as she was. But Taryn? Taryn had called her beautiful.

As she walked outside, she could hear the house sobbing. Painful, howling sounds bellowed within the confines of her head. It was ear splitting and it was strange to think no one else could hear it. Shaky hands met her driver side door handle, and she yanked it open and hurried inside. Settling the bag in the passenger seat, she locked her hands on the wheel and stared back at the home.

It didn't look run down anymore. Nothing was loose or hanging off. The color on the outside didn't look faded anymore. Even the yard looked clearer. The whimpering of the house was getting to be too much for Taryn. Turning on the car and backing out of the driveway, she didn't even make it out of the neighborhood before she was throwing up in her lap. Her body hurt and she felt like her veins had acid coursing through them.

Her eyes burned and she felt her stomach flipping at the threat of emptying once more. This weird bout of illness couldn't be ignored, but she wasn't far enough away yet. She needed to find someplace safe to be, to park. Instead, the further she drove the worst she felt. She threw up three more times until there was blood splatter on her legs.

Sobbing uncontrollably, she didn't know what it was that told her to turn around. Maybe it was a weird test. She needed to see if being away from the house was the cause, or if it was just all the nerves and fear getting at her. *Has the connection I first felt to the house grown into some sort of physical bond?*

It took fifteen minutes to get back to the driveway, and she noticed right away the work van was gone. It was nowhere to be found. Curiosity got the better of her. The feeling in her stomach was settled and nothing hurt anymore. *This isn't real life. This shit doesn't exist.* Disbelief turned around as she managed to go through the front door. The house looked even better. The stench of her own vomit wafting up to her nose and making her scrunch her face. Walking through the door, she went to look at her bedroom again. The wall and carpet were completely cleaned. There was no trace of body parts, gore, or anything.

Taryn sat on the floor in her bedroom and curled into a ball, beginning to sob uncontrollably. The house had clearly gotten rid of the evidence. *Now there's no reason to worry about someone finding out, right? Will I be able to live like this? Is my car really my only other option?* As scared as she was, she stayed put. Ending up on her side, she let the overwhelming emotions about her situation lull her to sleep.

<u>Mutually Beneficial</u>

When Taryn woke up, she was in the same uncomfortable place on the floor, covered in puke still. As she sat up, she looked around and took a deep breath. Okay. she thought to herself. Standing up, she went to the bathroom and started the shower. She needed to clean herself up and get into fresh clothes. The house had told her she was safe, and while most people would have laughed at the notion or ran for the hills, she believed it.

The house felt at ease with Taryn inside her. She pushed the hot water through the pipes, giving Taryn the relaxation she needed. They belonged together. She'd show her that. Somehow.

After the shower, Taryn cleaned up her clothes and the carpet. In clean clothes and feeling far more like her usual self, she paced around the kitchen. The things she heard from the house were few and far between. Most of which, if she were honest, were just feelings she got. They had to have come from somewhere though. Maybe it was just her lack of desire to live on the streets. Things were supposed to start looking up.

"How do we do this?" She asked out loud, almost wanting a physical being to appear in front of her to have this lengthy conversation with. Instead there was a shifting sound and then nothing. "I can't just bring you people to eat... what will you do if I'm all there is?"

Safe. You.

A heavy sigh escaped Taryn and she shook her head. "I don't think I can stay here like this... I can't kill people!" Taryn was trying to control the tone of her voice but it was getting more difficult.

Please.

The loneliness the house felt at the thought of Taryn leaving was unbearable. How could she make her understand? She was safe here.

"I need an answer. Do I have to bring people to you? Is that what you need?" It was difficult not having something specific to look at, so she just resorted to looking around a lot.

Yes.

"I don't have it in me to be a murderer. I can't do what you need." Taryn's voice was low now, tears rolling out of her eyes. She hated this feeling of powerlessness. This was supposed to be a fresh start. A way to start over and do the right thing.

Please.

Every time the house begged, Taryn felt like her heart was going to break. Her emotions felt so real to Taryn. She knew these feelings so well. Begging for someone, anyone, to love her. To treasure her and to see the good in her. She had done this so many times with her family. With friends. With partners. Still, she had ended up completely empty-handed.

Lonely.

Swallowing the lump in her throat, her eyes were red from tears as the house seemed to whimper around her through the sounds of expanding pipes. Nodding, she didn't know how to respond. "Yes. I'm lonely." She finally said.

We.

Taryn sputtered out her emotions then, shaking as she felt the weight of it all coming down on top of her. "Yes. We're lonely." The words felt natural and Taryn felt so much pain with this house. She was just as sad as Taryn.

"I don't know how to do this. I don't know how to bring you human beings. I don't know how to get away with this." She was staring down at her torn nails, as she plucked at them. Maybe if she stared at them long enough, she'd think of a solution.

Please.

Taryn closed her eyes, her face hot and her lips raw from chewing on them as she sobbed. "Okay. Okay." She mumbled the response. She had no idea how this was going to work, but maybe they could be good for each other. Neither one wanted to plead for love anymore. Neither one wanted to be alone. If she could find a way to help this house, then the house could help her. They could be what each other needed. The house could protect Taryn, and Taryn could love and appreciate this house. There were no clear answers, but living inside a house that loved you, sure beat the hell out of living in a world where no one else would.

A WARNING DISMISSED

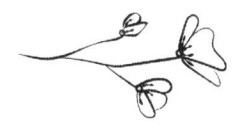

The following footage was transcribed from footage collected from the home of missing Cecelia Lyman, a twenty-six year old woman who went missing November 13th 2022.

```
Camera One - Office
11/12/2022
9:45 P.M.
```

I'm Cici. How cliche, right? Sitting in the office, talking to a camera, about to explain how I feel documenting is somehow going to make me feel less crazy. It won't. The truth is, I'm only doing it in hopes of someone finding these and burning this house to the ground. I've been here for three months, and it has been the most exhausting three months of my life. I'm in tears as I film this. I'm shaking. My entire body is locked up, knowing at any moment something is going to happen.

```
Camera Three - Living Room
11/12/2022
9:47 P.M.
```

From the living room camera, it can be seen that each cabinet door in the kitchen opens slowly all at once. They remain open for just a moment before all slamming shut at the same time.

```
Camera One - Office
11/12/2022
9:47 P.M.
```

Fuck! That was the kitchen cabinets. Again. One night they did this for hours. Just open and shut. Open and shut. It is maddening. Some days I'm not even scared anymore, just irritated. I can't sleep and I can't seem to get away from here long enough to find rest anywhere else. You can see the bags under my eyes. My cheeks are sunken in. I can barely eat or breathe, I'm so jumpy. Just a giant mess.

When I first moved here, I knew right away something was off but I had to find a place and quick. At first it was little things. Coming into a room and something is somewhere I didn't leave it. Or, the lights might act a bit funny. Sometimes, the fridge would be opened, and I was certain I had closed it. Noises in the middle of the night and sometimes I thought I was hearing whispering.

Then it got worse. Brand new food would suddenly be rotten. I would feel my hair being tugged. The whispering turned into low grumbles, saying my name. 'Cici. Cici.' Over and over. I began to be plagued by nightmares. Something sitting at the edge of my bed. Or something crawling on the ceiling from inside my closet. The nightmares turned into suicidal imaginings and I knew I needed to get help.

```
Camera Four - Hallway
11/12/2022
9:56 P.M.
```

The lights flicker in the hall and the walls appear to pulse in the darkness with decay. Each time the light dims, the paint seems to peel off the wall. When the lights are stable again, everything looks normal. A faint shadow appears in the entry from the hall to the office where Cici is sitting.

```
Camera One - Office
11/12/2022
9:57 P.M.
```

Did you see that? The lights? And sometimes this house looks like it is falling apart. Like, maybe it was in a fire? Or something else happened. I don't fucking know anymore! I'm trying to take a deep breath. Shit! I'm just going to do what I always do. Close my eyes and breathe.

```
Camera Four - Hallway
11/12/2022
9:59 P.M.
```

Lighting returns to normal in the hallway and there is no other movement.

```
Camera Two - Bedroom
11/13/2022
12:16 A.M
```

Cici lies in her bed. Tossing and turning.

```
Camera One - Office
11/13/2022
3:08 A.M.
```

I couldn't sleep. Talking to myself makes me feel some weird sense of comfort. I had bad dreams again, which is nothing new.

```
Camera Two - Bedroom
11/13/2022
3:08 A.M.
```

Light flickers on in the bedroom and the closet door opens. Wobbling to and from for a moment, it slams shut, causing a picture to fall off the wall just as the lights go out.

```
Camera One - Office
11/13/2022
3:09 A.M.
```

What the fuck? I'm so tired of this. I can't stand living this way!

Banging erupts around Cici and items from the desk and bookshelves clatter to the ground as she covers her face into her knees.

Stop! Stop! *Stop!*

```
Camera One - Office
11/13/2022
```

1:00 P.M.

I managed to get an hour or two of sleep but I feel my sanity withering away. I never thought this sort of thing would happen to me and now that I'm stuck in this situation, I don't know what else to do. I looked into this house right after the first occurrences and I can't find anything to explain why things would be weird here. I need answers. I want to know if I leave, will it follow? Honestly, staying at my parents at this age isn't ideal, but I don't know what the fuck else to do. I don't want to put this on someone else either.

```
Camera Two - Bedroom
11/13/2022
1:04 P.M.
```

The closet door opens slowly. The light inside flickering off and on, revealing a dark figure knelt on the top shelf of the closet. The figure is gone after the light remains on.

The lights flash one more time and now the figure is crawling out of the closet on the ceiling. It moves towards the camera and the screen turns black.

```
Ring Camera - Front Porch
11/13/2022
1:05 P.M.
```

Woman approaches and pushes the button. Backing up from the door, she looks over the space and seems to hesitate coming closer to the door. Her physical stance looks uncomfortable.

```
Camera One - Office
11/13/2022
```

1:05 P.M.

Cici checks her phone before looking back up at the camera.

Someone is here... I have no idea who this is.

Cici leaves camera running.

**Ring Camera - Front Porch
11/13/2022
1:07 P.M.**

Cici: Hi, can I help you?

Stranger: Uh, this is, I shouldn't have come but I keep... I keep seeing you and this house.

Cici: I'm sorry? Who are you?

Stranger: My name is Belle. I'm a psychic medium. I work in the next town over and for the last several nights I... are you having troubles here?

Cici: I'm sorry, I don't know what this is about...

Stranger: I'm sorry. I know this is confusing. I'm here because I think you're in danger. I think you know what I'm talking about.

Cici: I... think so. Would you want to come inside?

Belle: No.

Belle is seen on camera backing away from the front door.

Cici: Okay well then what did you come here for?

Belle: To tell you that there is a really good chance you won't be alive tomorrow morning."

Cici: What the fuck, lady?

Belle hurries back to her car and rushes to get away from Cici's house.

```
Camera One - Office
11/13/2022
1:12 P.M.
```

Cici appears back in front of the camera visibly shaken, with tears coming out of her eyes.

I don't know what the fuck that was. What's the point? She came here to tell me I'm going to die? Why? She wasn't going to help, she had nothing else to say.

```
Camera Three - Living Room
11/13/2022
1:13 P.M.
```

From the living room camera, the walls begin to change. Slowly, everything ages and begins to fall apart. Cabinet doors peel, hanging from their hinges. The floor looks rotted and has numerous holes. The furniture in the living room looks eaten through and burned. Everything looks dated and torn apart.

```
Camera One - Office
11/13/2022
1:13 P.M.
```

I don't fucking know what to do. I'm just going to go to my parents. Maybe there I'll at least get sleep? Maybe it really is *just* this fucking house. I need something to bring me back to sanity. Something to give me peace.

Cici cuts camera.

```
Camera Four - Hallway
11/13/2022
1:14 P.M.
```

Camera shows decay seeping into the structure of the hallway. Looking into the office, Cici stands and exits the room, not noticing everywhere around is rot. She can be seen going into her bedroom. A faint outline of a figure is seen walking behind her. Slowly it moves.

```
Camera Two - Bedroom
11/13/2022
1:14 P.M.
```

Cici goes into her closet to retrieve a bag and puts it on her bed. Tossing miscellaneous items she needs inside, she is frantic in her movement. The bedroom is beginning to deteriorate on camera, but Cici still hasn't noticed. As she goes into the closet to get clothing, the door slams shut. The figure from the hall approaches the door and vanishes into the cracked threshold.

```
Camera Two - Bedroom
11/13/2022
```

1:42 P.M.

The closet door opens and the light inside flickers. Fingers can be seen gripping the top of the frame. Outstretched fingers show hands and then arms. A bloodied figure emerges, flailing as though held by an invisible string. Cici's mouth is open in a scream but the camera picks up no sound.

The footage shows her mangled corpse being drug slowly, yet aggressively, across the ceiling from the closet until she can no longer be seen at all. A bloody trail is all that remains after only a few seconds. The closet light shuts off for good, and the door slams shut.

A Little Mad

The shrillness of the voice.

Something no one could forget.

In a dream such as this, the subject is completely unaware of their state of mind. Unaware that the images they are seeing are sickening sludgy pieces of their subdued consciousness. Wakeful tendencies are no longer accounted for, and the very idea of control has lapsed into an alternate reality.

No.

There'd be no waking from this nightmare. The terrors. The screams. Neill found himself in a large, poorly lit room. It was littered with medicine trays and surgical carts. Various machines made noises that sounded like they were underwater. There were beds with bloody sheets and battered padding. Separated, but barely, by large white screens on wheels. The metal of the beds rusted over, and miscellaneous nuts and bolts were scattered like confetti all over the broken, dingy tiles.

The smell of mildew swam down his throat and into his lungs. How could anyone think they were asleep? As he pushed back the screens, he found no one. Not a single person that had a purpose there, or someone who could tell him what *his* purpose was. His strained vision bounced over knocked over beds, blood splattered cotton, and emptied syringes. A crunching sound beneath his bare foot told him he had stepped on one. Pain surged through the arch of his foot, and he lifted it to examine the damage. "Goddamn it," he groaned.

Small droplets of blood fell to the floor, and he tried to pick out any remnants of the glass. It was difficult to see what he was doing. Trying to remember that this wasn't real, he forced himself to put his foot down. *I have to just keep moving until I wake up.* There was no point in lingering in a world that would cease to exist come morning.

Only it did exist. It waited for him. Every night, he was lulled to sleep, and found himself in a place similar to this. Sometimes it was a field piled high with rotting corpses. In that one, the bodies would roll off each other. Pieces of flesh and left over tissue would clump together and yank free of the skeleton. They'd crawl towards him, begging. Pleading. Asking him to help. To undo all the damage done.

Other times, he would find himself in a library. The stacks would be abnormally tall, towering over him. Dusty books would fall periodically to clatter at his feet. Each page would reveal a picture of torment. Women, children, and even animals. Ripped to shreds. Pinned by medical instruments in a way that one might take note of their insides. Then, just as he'd find his courage to close the book, the people and creatures would come to life. They'd flood the page and come crawling out, begging for him to help them.

The hospital was new, though. Perhaps that was why it was so unsettling. Despite being new, the little details rang too familiar. The dark green drapes that hung just a little too short over the windows. The pattern in the tile that didn't line up because the job was done poorly. His eyes scanned and counted. Ten beds. He counted again. Still ten.

There were sinks on either side of the large space. This nightmare had it down to even the color of paintings hung around that were meant to bring cheer to the dying. Neill's subconscious had done a lot to him over the years, but this was starting to feel like something more. This felt too real. It felt too comfortable. The pain in his foot was *real*. He could feel the sharpness of the leftover shards as he stepped forward.

As he found himself looking over the last bed, the sound erupted again. Vibrating off the walls around him and reverberating inside his mind. "No!" Over and over again, the response to an unknown action took place. He was lost. Putting his hands over his ears, he groaned. "Where are you?" Then there was silence. There was no sound to be heard.

Shakily putting his hand up to the last sheet, separating him from the last bed, he pulled it away. The moment his fingers met the metal of the rack that held the moveable wall, the scream pushed him back and he fell backwards into the previous bed. "Shit..." he said, forcing himself back to his feet. This time he didn't want to waste any time. Jerking the sheet back so hard it rattled as it clattered to the ground. The sound startled him and caused him to jump. He let out a rushed laugh through his clenched teeth.

There was an eerie echo that followed his own laugh. Neill dropped his smiling expression and slowly turned his head in the direction of the sound. There was a stressed lump that had arrived in his throat, and suddenly he was perspiring on his forehead. Up on the bed, staring right at him with only one good eye, was a girl. She sat erect, her legs, presumably, facing away from her, and her head tilted as she gawked at him. Her hair was covered in a thick red substance, caked onto the parts of her porcelain skin that remained intact. The good eye was a dark brown, splattered with violent tinges of red around the iris. Her neck cracked as she turned to face him, and Neill's hand was instantly rising to cover his gaping mouth.

A horrified breath crept through the creases of his fingers. Her other eye was nonexistent. It had been replaced with a large black button. The edges of where it met her flesh were sewn with a neon green string. The girl's cheeks were pinned high on her face, with large industrial strength staples. The mouth that had been letting out the cries, was replaced with a rusty, metallic zipper. Large and tearing at the seams.

She shuttered and Neill moved closer to her. His hand stretched for her, but he was hesitant to get any closer. "Are you...?" He thought over the best way to approach the girl. Whoever had done this was a monster. A mad man. He deserved the same fate. Or worse. He couldn't even find her legs beneath the sheets, as his eyes rocketed over every inch of this mangled body. "Are you okay?" He offered a gentle tone as he was now inches from her body.

A small tear escaped the girl's tear duct and slipped over her bloodied cheek. "Can I...?" But before he could even offer any type of help, he was already flying away from her. Her zipper opened, and that same ear splitting sound was escaping her lips. The sort of scream you wouldn't believe a human being was capable of. How could one sound hold so many emotions? Fear? Anguish? Despair? Emptiness?

Ripped from the nightmare, Neill's body jolted to life. Reality. The heavy realization struck that she wasn't just afraid, she was afraid of *him*. His hands lay flat on the bed and clenching at the sheets. Covered in his own pool of sweat, he was still screaming for several moments before he was able to control himself.

Running his fingers through his hair, he gripped at the soaked strands. "Why..." he started to say, but didn't bother to finish, unable to control the sobs that escaped his lips instead. He was at a loss. Complete and utter loss.

He had begun, long ago now it seemed, to make his own concoctions to help him sleep. Help him forget. Help release the tension that was inside him. So once again, as he had done for so many countless nights, he was forcing his naked body from the discomfort he found in his own bed. Crossing the thresholds of his home, he found himself inside the kitchen. Trash and old food containers everywhere. Cleanliness wasn't at the top of his priority list anymore. Between the girl locked in his makeshift lab, and running on little sleep, there were more important things to worry about than household chores.

Opening up the different cabinets, he let his uneasy fingers fumble around over the different labeled glass jars. Some were bigger than others. Some only have a small vial in a plastic holder. "Fuck." He felt his fist slam into the weak surface of the counter. He jerked his head up as though a light bulb had proceeded to go off. "Right..." he answered himself and went to the lower cabinets. Pulling out three jars, he jerked off the tops. Neill found his mortar and pestle. Taking out different amounts of his three ingredients, he added each individually to his bowl.

1. Schisandra

2. Buspirone

3. Halcion

Each one contributed an element to the concoction he needed. The berries of Schisandra he would use as a type of sedative. The buspirone for anxiety. And the Halcion, naturally, would help him go to sleep. Though the Halcion had created a bit of a dependency, he didn't care. He was hooked on so many different things, the last thing he cared about was getting rid of one that would allow him a little rest. Forcing the ingredients into his bowl, he rubbed them together repeatedly until they were of the right texture. Pulling out a bottle of water, he poured it into a small cup. Not bothering to dilute the mix, Neill added the herbs to the water. A few spins of his glass and he would down the entire contents of his glass.

Forcing himself to swallow the disgusting mix, he cleared his throat heavily. Quickly reaching for a bottle of gin, which was naturally very low in liquor, he took a quick swig to rid himself of the taste. He found himself sitting at the broken table not too far from where he had been standing. Slumping down, he caught his face in his hands. He would probably crash right there on the shitty wood.

"Her face..." he could still see it, crystal clear. And though in his dream he had wondered who had done it to her, he knew in this world it had been him. The great and wonderful Dr. Mitchum. Allowing his face to slam into the table, he only groaned from the contact. "There has to be a way to forget what I've done." His voice was barely audible.

When the hum inside his mind stopped, he could hear a subtle sound coming from his lab. Sighing, he forced his body up, already feeling the effects of the drink he had made. Between the lack of sleep, the drug induced state, and the slam of his head against the table; he stumbled over to the icebox. Opening it quickly, he grabbed a few items and the bottle of water. "Feeding time." He said aloud, for no particular reason at all.

His legs were wobbly as he moved forward and found his way to the lock on his office door. Reaching for the key above the frame, he pulled it down and unlocked it. There was no light in the room and he slid inside not bothering to turn it on just yet. As the door closed behind him, he instantly thought back to the girl with the zipper for a mouth. "I'm just as much a monster now as I was then." The only thing left to hear in that moment was a laugh that expelled from his raspy throat. The laugh ranged in tones as well as volume. It would appear to most that he had in fact completely lost his mind. Crazed by his past, and what he had been forced to do. The things he was still doing. Crazed, indeed. A monster. Insane. Lunatic. Mad.

THERE IS ONLY US

I WOULD HAVE NEVER thought it was possible to be inside someone's dreams. To see what they see and feel what they feel. To be inside someone's head and not be the one in control. To exist in a mind that is foreign to me. It can be a truly exhilarating experience, until the dreams turn into nightmares.

I can't recall the first time it ever happened. It might have been after our first kiss. It might have been after the first time we made love. What I *do* remember is how vivid the dreams became. Ashlyn and I had only been together for a few weeks when our connection surpassed that of any lover I had ever known. I was drawn to her in a way words could never explain. Of course, when I met her, it was under a different name initially. She was introduced to me as someone she was not.

I once thought we were finally moving forward. That the world and all the hate that consumed it, was slowly diminishing. Bigotry and the violence were supposed to be dying out. I never felt so naïve as I did when I realized how truly alive that hatred was. How truly dangerous it was; and it was only going to get worse.

"Long night?" I hear Ashlyn speak, her fingers grazing my bare shoulders as she glides into the room. I don't answer outright. I usually don't have to. "More dreams," she says. It falls as a statement rather than a question.

"I prefer the dreams you have about me." I smile, she smiles back. Her nose brushes mine just before she kisses me.

She lingers for a moment. The kiss turns almost eager as her fingers move across my collarbone and down between my breasts. We've done this a thousand times, and yet my breath hitches as though I've never known her touch. I swallow hard and she leans back. In perfect unison, we both sigh softly.

See, Ashlyn is a bit of a empath. When I first met her, she offered to do a tarot reading for me. At the time, I didn't quite know what I believed as far as tarot. I wasn't sure I knew what I believed about anything. There was something about her that pulled me in, though. Something that made me want to know her and be a part of her life. The tarot reading was so spot on, I grew more intrigued.

I'm pulled back to the present moment by a cup sliding into my hands. The milky color makes me smile. In so many ways, we always say we were like the same person. As she sits across from me with her black coffee, I smirk to think we are not. I can tell she remembers the gruesome details of her dream simply by her lack of words.

I notice quickly there is no remorse or sadness in her eyes. Instead, she seems at peace. Just sitting across from me, happy to be here. Perhaps this should be a daunting display, but it isn't. I trust Ash with my life, and I could never think ill of her.

"Who were they?" I ask. The details hang like a wet cloth in the space between us at the table. Ashlyn shakes her head. I frown.

When Ashlyn told me who she really was, I had to learn a different type of respect for her thoughts. Coming out as a transgender woman to someone who wants to date you could not have been an easy task. Even after two years, I find myself cringing to think of what she must have felt during that time.

I will never fully understand the stress and strain it must have put on her mind. Waiting at any moment for me to abandon her. Only that wasn't what happened at all. Instead, it was all too easy to want to keep her in my life. See, even from the first time she told me, I knew I'd spend the rest of my life protecting her. I'd burn this earth into nothing, if it meant keeping her safe.

Trust is balanced and nurtured carefully in our relationship. So, if she doesn't want to discuss her dreams now, I trust there was a reason. Honestly, it's something I'm still working on. It had become natural to just expect a partner to tell me everything on a whim. Learning to allow space and time was something my therapist said we'd definitely keep working on. The thought almost makes me smile.

I make it most of the way through my shift before I realize how distracting that dream really was. I had spent the day typing on a keyboard and making small talk with people about things I know I didn't care about. I had eaten a sandwich at my desk, while still answering emails. I was on autopilot, but that dream played in my head on repeat.

Now that I have been awake for so long, I can't remember as many of the details. When Ash's dreams are good and full of wonder, I remember them beautifully. I often joke that I wonder if she has a gift she's unaware of. The ability to make people feel good by pushing imagery into their minds. In truth though, a big part of me is glad this isn't one of the times I remembered everything.

I could hear the screaming. I could see blood splashing up, and all over the room. Body parts and gore littered the pictures in my head. Who were those people? Did Ashlyn know them? I knew a great deal about her life, but I was pretty certain she hadn't experienced a trauma regarding murder.

As I gather my things to leave for the day, I decide to ask her again once I get home. I want to know more about what I had seen, and she was the only person with the ability to help me better understand. We had messaged throughout most of the day except for once a few hours into the morning when her replies had slowed. She had work to do, so I dismissed all the worry I had. I love Ashlyn, and I was almost certain she was not capable of the things I saw in that dream. Almost.

Truly the most exciting parts of my life are my homelife. Most days it feels like I'm rushing through the mundane just to get back to Ash. She lights up any room she's in. With the ability to turn colors from gray to vibrant sherbets, she's the only thing I look forward to. We often discuss finding something in a career that interests me, but there is no such career. I'm motivated by a job. I'm still finding my own creative path, and right now the most important thing to me is the life we're building with each other. Perhaps that's the romantic in me. Or, some might say, the child.

As I make my way back to the apartment, I can tell from down the hall that the door is opened. My steps falter, and I lean out to see if I can see inside. Through the crack, there appears to be no light and I'm trying to control the panic clenching at my intestines. My head goes to a dark place. Immediately, I picture Ashlyn's corpse lying in our bed. Slashed open and nude. Something vulgar on the walls with her blood.

'The world isn't safe for people like us.' I remember Ash saying to me the first time we were ever bothered in public.

I only allow myself one more moment to get myself together before I go to gently push the door open. It is pitch black on the inside of our apartment. The only light provided is from the threshold I'm now standing in. "Ash?" I whisper. Nothing.

Being a woman, I learned a long time ago to carry constant distrust with me. Distrust of the world around me and all the people in it. Being in a relationship with a woman, who also happened to be transgender, the walls grew taller and my circle smaller. I felt I not only had to protect myself now, but also the woman I love.

'The world isn't safe for people like us.' I hear her words again, as though she has whispered them into my flesh, just beneath my ear. Why were there tears in my eyes?

My hand reaches out to connect with the bar next to the kitchen. There isn't anything I can think of to grab that might work as a weapon. Although things were moving disgustingly slow, I did all I could to move them faster. So, I did what they taught us to do. I took my keys and pushed them outwards between my knuckles. It wouldn't maim or murder, but it would be enough to get someone off me. If it was good enough to do when walking to my car at night, surely it would help here?

I hear a shuffling in the apartment, and everything feels infinitely darker. My heart is racing. I can feel the tingle of it throughout my entire body. The tears that were blurring my vision, are now sliding down my cheeks. "Ash?" I whisper again.

The next thing I hear is footsteps. Pacing, I think, back and forth. I move slower around the apartment. The space that was just a refuge not ten hours ago. I should have called the cops, but I was worried I was overreacting. Isn't that what we're always doing as women? Our feelings never justified, only over amplified? I'm cursing myself for this now.

I'm going to be so angry with myself if something had happened to her because I was too worried about calling the police. If I let society tell me when to show concern and when to keep it inside. I find the anger is giving me strength, and I'm able to keep moving. I feel less frozen, and this time, more prepared to help the woman I love.

I finally make it almost to the bedroom. I have my keys raised just as a shadow crosses in front of me. Immediately, I close my eyes and sigh in relief. It was just Ashlyn. The light in the bedroom is minimal as she moves back and forth in silence.

Several seconds pass, as I attempt to come out of my overly panicked state. The fear and concern is still there, but I feel the ringing in my ears dull to a quiet pulse. My heart, well, there's nothing I can do to help that at the moment.

Lowering my hand, I reach inside the room to flip on the switch. Watching Ashlyn, she moves in a weakened state to face me. The front of her blouse is covered in blood. Her makeup is smeared with tears and her cheeks are stained red. I'm frozen again. I give up steadying my breathing.. I can't speak.

There is no allowing her space for long before I have to close the distance between us. I use my thumbs to wipe her tears, which only smudges the dried blood onto my hands. "What happened baby?" I'm an emotional mess. Who hurt her? Did it happen in our home? How bad was it? The exaggerated thoughts from before amplify to dangerous levels now.

As she sobs with my hands on her face, there is a sinking feeling in my gut. I couldn't protect her.

I wasn't here and someone got in.

I wasn't with her, and someone attacked her outside.

While the thoughts are spiraling into an unsafe place, I realize I haven't seen any wounds yet. It should comfort me, but instead it makes me dread where they might be.

"I-i-it," she stammers, "i-it isn't my blood." The words hold physical weight as they slam into my body and force me to take a step back.

"Okay," I say, far more calmly than I would have thought I was capable of.

My hands touch her shoulders, and I encourage her to sit down. I sit down on the floor in front of her, trying my best to keep physical contact. It is something we often do in harder conversations. It works as a tether of sorts, keeping us bound to the reality that we are still here with each other.

Her sobbing has only eased slightly by the time our eyes meet. Those beautiful green and amber hues are made only brighter by her tears. I can feel it in my heart. Whatever she did, whomever she hurt, I won't care. I'll know it was justified and I'll stand beside her.

I reach over and touch her hands. This is when I realize they, too, are covered in blood. Thick and caked on. Parts of it feel like scabs all over her once supple skin. I can feel my heart skip a beat. I'm scared. I'm not getting information fast enough. I'm worried. Is there someone still in our apartment?

"I'll show you." Her words take me by surprise. The alarming sound of her confidence knocks the wind out of my lungs.

I only give her a nod. Her hands press into my temples as I feel my head jolt back and my body lock into position.

The image I see is just like the dream I saw the night before. There is a decent sized brick building with white shutters and a wrap-around porch. Flowers are hanging in planters almost all the way around, which match perfectly the ones planted in the ground. All the furniture on the porch is the same with detailed seat cushions that carry the same purple coloration as the flowers.

There are a few cars parked in the driveway, but I don't recognize any of them. I don't remember there being cars in the dream. As I take a second look, I notice they are falling apart. Rust and missing parts. Flat tires and shattered mirrors.

I move forward, but not on my own accord. The front door of the house opens, and I'm shot inside, as if snatched by some invisible rope. The sensation is confusing, because I can also still feel Ashlyn's hands on the side of my face. Her skin on mine is the only reason I feel safe. She is, and will always be, my safety.

The inside of the house moves in a blur, and I can barely tell which rooms I am moving through. I can hear chattering and even someone yelling. It feels like there is a fog in my mind, but I'm familiar with it. Ashlyn's memories are guiding me. Soon, this will all make sense. I'll see what horrible thing left Ash with no choice but to hurt another human being.

My body is yanked one last time forward and then immediately backwards in a harsh whiplash I am not prepared for. I cough out a response, but there is no noise. I'm merely a spectator. As my vision focuses, I can tell I'm in a dimly lit bedroom.

There are people sitting around, as if around an imaginary camp fire. They are moving their arms in an exaggerated manner, and shouting over each other. At first it is just loud noise manifesting physically, and vibrating around me. I can't tell what they're saying. Then the words became clearer.

"Faggot."

"Trans monsters."

"He-shes!"

My heart pounds harder and harder by the second. What is this? The faces are blurred, and I struggle to make out any distinction between them. Then, all at once, the noise stops. Confusion takes over the anger, and they all turn and look at me. Frozen and scared, all I can think is 'Fuck, can they see me?' This has never happened before. Am I in danger?

Before I can call out to question it, I realize they are looking through me. Turning over my shoulder, I see her. Ashlyn. Bold and beautiful. She stands in the door and says nothing. Chaos and whimsy surround her. Confused by what I see, all I can do is stand there.

At first, nothing happens. Then, I hear screaming erupt from behind me. Turning from my lover, I face the cacophony of horror. In the center of the circle is what looks like the standing remains of a once human being. The other patrons are splattered with blood, as though this person exploded from the inside. Their mangled corpse takes time to collapse to the ground.

Wet, juicy viscera clings to people as they sputter and remain motionless. They seem unable to move or speak. 'She is captivating, isn't she?' I think slyly to myself.

My mouth hangs open and I watch as Ash advances. She walks right through me, a chill running up and down my spine. Something in me tells me to close my eyes, but in my head, I hear her voice *'Don't.'* So I don't. I look on as the woman I lay beside every night begins to work her way through the group of people in the brick house.

The first one she reaches; she wastes no time. Shoving both of her thumbs into their eyes, the screaming grows louder and hoarser. At first nothing came out. Ashlyn presses and presses until an odd color of goop and red squirts out over her extremities. She doesn't even close her own eyes. There is no hesitation or guilt upon her features. All I can see is her focus and purpose.

I'm recalling now the crusted nature of her fingers and realizing that it was not just blood. Ooze from the eyes had caked into the wrinkles of her knuckles. It had solidified in the beds of her nails. Still, as I want to snap my lids shut, all I hear is *'Don't.'* So, I watch.

As I watch Ashlyn find another person, someone came from behind her. I try to call out, but she doesn't need my help. Her hand lifts and twists, and in one effortless movement the person is bent in half. Folded up like a metal chair, and then they collide with the ground in a loud 'thud'.

My eyes are stinging with tears, and I can't look up from the man on the ground. I can't tell what I am looking at, and wish I could just look away. The look on his face is utter fear, I'm not even sure he has time to feel pain. Maybe

Ashlyn was making it easier for me to see, or if I was just getting better at focusing while in this state.

By the time I look up, many others have fled. I hear loud screaming from another room, and I can see that Ash is pointing in the direction of the chaos. I don't know what she is doing to those people, but I'm not sure I could handle knowing.

The emotions that flood me are not of fear, per say. I feel fear for the other people. Fear of dying in a way that won't ultimately change their mind. I fear that they will have peace in death, and never know pain or suffering again. That they'll leave this place, having broken the spirits of who knows how many in our community, and have only suffered a short time. But not Ash. Not the woman I love. I will never fear her.

The noises around me are slowly becoming muted. The far away sounds have faded to nothing and there are only those who are physically close to me left to hear. Ashlyn uses her open palm to push a woman clear across the room. Her thick body slams hard against a table, causing it to collapse beneath her. The female voice is clearly in agony. Ash draws closer, but the woman has no strength in her to try and get away. Both she and my lover are covered in blood.

Ashlyn grows closer still, and picks up a piece of that broken table. I try to step closer. I wanted to tell her they have had enough. I want to beg her to come home with me. I want us to leave this behind us.

In truth, I do not carry any sorrow for these people. I have known hate all my life and so has my partner. It might be better to speculate, instead, that I was growing uncomfortable with *how* comfortable I am with this. That I don't harbor any regret. I carry no guilt in my belly and no sadness in my heart. They asked for this. Over and over with their bigotry. Perhaps they ought to have planned their exit strategy more carefully before they threw stones at a witch.

The thoughts go silent as a loud ringing in my ears takes over in a high pitch. I lift my hands to cover them, but it does nothing to shield me from the frequency. This happens to me sometimes when I'm in Ash's head for too long. This scene was painfully slow in some ways, and not slow enough in others. I watch as

Ash lifts her hands above her head and plunges the wooden piece down into the woman's abdomen.

She does this again. And again. And one more time.

My body is shaking. I can taste the bitter spit in my mouth, collecting at the threat of vomit. I watch her cut a circle over and over until she is pulling out body parts I am unable to identify. Gory, sopping pieces splash up against the woman's chest and Ashlyn takes her time before seemingly accomplishing what she had hoped.

Dropping the splintered wood, I can hardly hear it through the screaming in my head. Completely mesmerized by her, I watch her stand. Blood flows down her arms and fingers, smacking against the body and the floor beneath her. Spatter of ichor adds to the dots next to the freckles on her cheeks. The stirring in my body creates a reaction I couldn't have controlled if I wanted to. How can I think about how beautiful she looks right now? How passionate and loving she is? How badly she deserves to feel this form of retribution? Why am I thinking about the next time I'll feel her hands on my body or her tongue in my mouth? My thoughts are racing and I wonder how much longer I'll be in this state.

I watch her spit at the body, for it is no longer a human being at this point. Leaning closer, I hear her with perfect clarity. She drowns out the sirens between my ears and all that is left is that voice I know to be my soulmate.

"By your definition," she pauses to flick blood down on the face of the corpse, "you're no longer a woman now either."

As if it had been spelled out in blood and female reproductive organs, I understand. Trans women, to people like this, aren't considered real women because they lacked the reproductive system to be one. Scoreboard, Ashlyn fucking one hundred. The bigots? Fucking zero.

I begin to recall all the times before when we were tormented for just wanting to live our lives. I remember the way people perceived me out in public with previous girlfriends. I remember the men assuming we were doing it for attention. Coming up to us and grabbing at us or calling out about offering something better.

'You just haven't met the right man.'

'Why don't we all go back to my place?'
'Only a real man knows how to satisfy a woman.'
'Your mouth is better suited for a cock.'

My anger is bubbling. My emotions are flying off the handle. I'm recalling the guy whose nose I broke, one night while out because he simply didn't take no for an answer. I remember all the things thrown at us when we'd go out on the streets too late.

Ashlyn had been bothered more than once by fake clients for her shop. Tarot drew in some pretty frustrating people sometimes. It wasn't until they saw the flag on her table or realized her voice sometimes went a little deeper when she was focused on her task. That was when their hate had grown loud. Amazing how bold they grow when their victim is alone.

We'd spent countless weekends cleaning off the spray paint. We repaired the broken windows. We'd hold each other for comfort.

One thing I always remember was wanting to inflict pain on the people who put her through this. Make it clear that if they wanted violence, they'd fucking get violence.

Tears stream down my face as I realize what this is. When I come to, I am sobbing uncontrollably in Ashlyn's lap. Her own pain continues as we hold each other. I am back in the now and all I can feel is relief that she has gotten rid of these people. Now, there are fewer people they'd hurt or cause trouble for.

It became clear as I watched the chaos unravel, this wasn't revenge. This was something *more*. This wasn't about these people in particular but about their mindset and those they could hurt. These were the people who viewed anyone in our community as a nuisance to society. We were a threat.

To what, I couldn't say. So maybe it's time we take it all back. Maybe it's time we become a true threat to bigotry and hate. How can we be the presumed 'monsters' when they want us all dead? Was that not worse?

Without realizing how much time has passed, I sit up and climb on top of Ashlyn. We push our bodies up onto the bed and my lips hungrily meet hers. I feel exhausted from the emotion, but aroused by the realizations. The blood and filth residue does not deter me from sitting up, and working my hands under the fabric of her shirt. I need skin to skin with her. I need to feel her close to me in a way I'd never want another human being.

My eyes lock with hers, and I sigh in need. "Were these people someone who hurt you?" She simply shook her head no. "You're safe with me." Something I've said every day since Ashlyn told me she was transgender. She smiles and sighs in the same way I had. "I love you so much."

The people from the dream hadn't come from a previous interaction. Instead, or so it appeared, the dream told her what to do. That her gifts and her visions would show her the ones who needed to be weeded out; gutted from society. These were not people who had harmed or bothered Ash personally, but they were people who needed to be eradicated.

I hear her reply 'I love you', and my lips lower to her belly. Kissing softly at the parts of her flesh caked in the outline of blood from her shirt. I lift the shirt in a manner that makes her lift up to pull it over her head. My hands gently slide over the soft material of her bra. Another sigh, this time from both of us.

"Tonight, there is only us. Tomorrow, we find a way to end them all." Ashlyn gives a simple smile and nods.

If they don't think we deserve the right to live, then they do not get that right either. We will take it from them. All of them. Just me and Ashlyn.

Alone

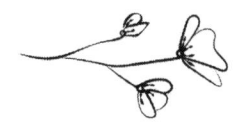

When it comes to death and funerals, I've never quite understood the energy put into them. I watched family members and friends get up at my aunt Althea's funeral and put on quite the performance. Pouring sentiments of what a wonderful human she was, and how kind natured she was soaked into all of us as I tried my best not to look indifferent. I didn't hate the woman, but we were far from being what I would consider "close." My mother, who had treated my aunt like an arch nemesis most of my life, was in shambles. I'd wager it had more to do with her own sense of mortality than actual remorse or sadness.

Afterwards, when I tried to leave, my mother begged me to stay with her 'I wish I could still ground you' eyes. Normally, I would have stuck to my guns and hightailed it out of there, but it was a death. It felt really inconsiderate to just leave. I was already harboring a lot of guilt for not feeling sad.

So I stayed. I walked around and mingled with a few people I recognized. I overheard a few of her friends discussing some gossip. I made eye contact with my mom a few times and she seemed to smile even once.

"Are you doing alright?" The voice wasn't one I recognized, but I turned to address it nonetheless.

"Oh, uh, yes. I'm fine, thanks."

My eyes rested on the source, a man I hadn't noticed before. He towered over me and stared down at me with a steel gaze. He was dressed nicely, and had his hair styled back. The top was a bit longer, but it was obvious he was keeping out of his face to be respectful. His jawline was sharp, and the smile he gave me made it hard not to smile back.

"How did you know her?" he asked, both of us glancing back to the viewing room.

"She was my aunt." His features shifted to a deep frown. "I wasn't very close to her. I'm really mostly here for my mom."

Though I could never admit it out loud, I felt nothing being in that room. I felt nothing seeing those people suffer a loss they deemed great. I felt nothing watching the woman who raised me suffer with her own convictions, now that her sister was dead and gone. I was merely a spectator. A ghost. Just along for the ride, pretending to be human. Pretending to feel things humans are supposed to feel.

"Well, I'm sorry for your loss." His voice was kind, and it was hard not to notice how warm his presence was.

"How about you? How did you know her?" Typical funeral small talk, something I didn't know if I was even up for.

"I didn't." My face must have shown my surprise, as he quickly chuckled and cleared his throat, "Well, I mean, I'm here for moral support."

"Ali?" I turned when I heard my mother calling me, nodding as I realized it was time to put on my own show.

"Duty calls." I smiled, and the stranger nodded in response.

I lasted about twenty more minutes before I was able to leave. The burial ceremony would be in the morning, but I already had excuses lined up to miss it. Thankfully it worked, because I couldn't handle another slew of these types of interactions. My social battery was completely depleted.

I was completely buried in my latest research project when my phone rang. It was my mother, but I had little energy to answer. After two more calls, I finally gave in. The woman on the other end of the line was a frantic mess. It took me several minutes to wrap my head around the words 'there was no body'.

Apparently someone really close to Althea, in a fit of dramatics, threw themselves onto the coffin before it was due to be put into the ground. Upon doing so, the cover slid down and revealed there was no body inside. Talk of a lawsuit and miscommunication were all I really gathered out of the rest of the conversation

"Why would she even be able to sue?" I asked, completely conflicted on my feelings regarding this conversation. I didn't have much to add and as selfish as it was, I didn't really care about the dilemma. I also knew it would be the worst thing I could do to my mother to be vocal about it.

"Well, Alissa, there was no body in the damn coffin! The owner gave some half ass excuse about mixing up paperwork and how her body must have ended up with another that was meant to be cremated." She was much more panicked and stressed than I was. It was her sister after all.

I always found the idea of bodies in the ground unsettling. It always felt like a very egotistical way to exist after you have passed on. I've never visited grave sites to mourn or talk to the dead. I've never understood why anyone does that. Perhaps it was that underlying pretentious need for comfort. As if a rotting corpse of someone you loved and cherished was something to be proud of. You spent all that money and time doing this pony show and they just aren't there anymore.

As my mother went on with her emotional tirade, I tried to remember that she needed me to agree. At this moment, she had called for validation. Well, validation and gossip. The truth was, my mother hated Althea. I wasn't the only one pretending my way through the funeral services. So I did the equivalent of nodding through a conversation. "Oh right. I understand. Of course. How tragic." The reality was, I just wanted to know where the body was.

Later that night, my phone rang. It was an old friend of mine who worked with the coroner's office.

"Griggs?" I was surprised he was calling, as late as it was. His voice was shaking on the other end and he could barely get out what he needed.

"Can you come to Landon Woods?" There wasn't much reason to hesitate, but I did. I couldn't help feeling like whatever he needed me to see was going to turn into something more than I was ready for. Maybe it was just the missing body that was on my mind.

"Sure. I'll be there in twenty."

I had worked with Griggs numerous times. During the day I was a textbook writer and at night a bit of a novelist. The textbooks paid the bills, and the novels fed into my insane appetite for the unexplained. I wrote about the things that went bump in the night. The only criteria was it had to be rooted in legends or folklore. My intrigue had started with notions of Nessie, Sasquatch, Mothman, and many others. These unexplainable things that had crept into the stories of cultures everywhere. Some versions were changed over the years and drastically depended upon which area of the continent you were in. Either way, whether it be the Skunk Ape of Florida or the Momo in Missouri, I studied and wrote about them all.

Griggs only ever called if shit got weird. Which meant, of course, shit got weird. Landon was not somewhere I frequented. There were up to fifty people who went missing in the dense woods every year. They were dark and thick and really hard to navigate. Always a source of interest, my ears were perked. I didn't live that far, and that made the ride to Landon giddy. I exited my truck, notebook shoved in my pocket, and went to find the coroner.

"Ali!" I heard the familiar voice and was instantly smiling. It was nice to feel something normal for a change.

Griggs was barely taller than me, and stood a little frumpy. He fit more of the detective stereotype than a coroner. We met when I used to manage a dry cleaners. He brought in uniforms and instantly became like an uncle to me. One conversation about stain management turned into conversations about life and family. We grew closer and as someone who didn't connect to people easily, it was really nice to have a friend. In fact, if not for Griggs, I probably wouldn't have gone to school to get my journalism degree or pursued writing of any kind.

The sky above us was pitch black, and the wind had picked up just a bit. There were cars everywhere. Lights flashed, highlighting the thick crowd gathered around the entry to the titan that was Landon Woods. People nodded in my direction, but no one really paid me much attention.

"Lot of people out here," I commented, looking around before giving Griggs a bear hug.

He leaned out of the hug and nodded "You'll see why…"

I was a bit surprised there was no briefing. Instead, he motioned with his fingers and nodded his head in the direction he wanted me to follow. My curiosity would have been clear on my features. I followed.

The silence around us was unexpected given how many cops and coats were around us. Nothing had been marked off yet, which was almost negligent, except that no one was likely to show up at Landon this late. I licked my lips and rolled them together, the darkness of the trees creeping over us and already making it difficult to see.

As if on cue, Griggs offered me a flashlight, which I was quick to turn on. "Are you going to say anything, or is this that bad?"

I didn't push as he took his time, clearly contemplating how to answer. "Well," he started, stopping in his steps and turning to face me, "I have no idea where to start." Griggs reoriented himself and started walking again. I did my best to keep stride.

"The beginning?" I shrugged, my light moving around to make sure I didn't hurt myself. I had worn boots, but those woods were tricky; night made it much more dangerous.

"I got a call about two hours ago, a body found in the woods. Okay, fine. No big deal." Griggs stopped to look around before deciding to turn slightly to the right. I noticed markers in the ground I hadn't seen before. It was getting darker the further we walked.

I waited for him to finish, and he wasn't saying anything. He was just walking and grunting. "Okay…" I prodded. His hesitation was driving me crazy.

"Well, so I get here, and yeah, there's a body. But it is in a hundred pieces. And the blood is splattered up trees. I mean…" There was another hesitation, but that time he stopped walking again. I tried to be patient, but I found myself drawing closer.

I was almost side by side with Griggs when his flashlight moved around the area in front of us. He didn't need to finish the thought. I could see it. The blood. The body parts. Everything was scattered in various directions. There were trails of blood leading up the trees. It was still shiny against the light of my friend's flashlight.

My face scrunched in response. I lifted my light to see Griggs, but he wasn't even blinking. I couldn't figure out why this is so upsetting to him. The blood patterns were a bit erratic, but not unlike others who get attacked by animals in the middle of the woods.

He used his free hand to wipe his brow, still shaking. Without knowing how else to show support, I put my hand on his shoulder. He shook his head.

"So, are you thinking an animal? I mean," I raised my light to look over the splatters again, "I have to admit these marks are a bit odd…"

I trailed off, and Griggs shook his head. "I just don't know anymore. Don't you have some answers? Bigfoot or Notchie?"

It was hard not to laugh. "You mean Nessie? That one is in water." I watched him for a moment before shaking my head. "Shit, I don't know. Do they know who it is yet?"

"Not yet. They took samples earlier. We'll know something soon."

I took a second to get closer to the mess, and I realized how hard it was to even differentiate some of the pieces. A heavy sigh left me as I wished I was able to help. Griggs didn't even believe in the stuff I wrote about, but I think it must have offered more reassurance than having no answers at all.

I stayed a little longer to work with Griggs. It was mostly conversation and spitting out wild theories about what could have happened. The cops came and went, most were unable to handle the scene. Small towns saw their fair share of blood and mayhem, but not much like this.

"Well, I guess call me tomorrow if you need anything? I know I can't offer much." Griggs and I exited the woods and started towards where I parked. "I think it is fair to assume that any animal living up here couldn't have done that though, not after a closer look. And I know it is a wild thing to consider..." I hesitated and he shook his head.

"Don't even say it, Ali. No way a human being did this."

"I don't know. Human beings are pretty awful." Griggs scoffed as if offended, "Psh, if you're in with me you're not human." I winked and hugged him to say goodbye. "Call me tomorrow." He nodded and did a salute.

As I pulled the truck back onto the road, my thoughts couldn't stop going back to the body in the woods. I immediately wanted to blame a human being for this. Logically, there weren't many animals in the area that could have done this. It didn't mean it *wasn't* an animal, but it was hard to not think outside the box on this. Bears could leave a lot of damage if they attacked a human, but it was more of a shredding with a very specific claw pattern. Wolves weren't in a habit of ripping and sloshing body parts while eating. Humans, on the other hand were capable of things like this, though usually there'd be a reason. Plus, I didn't have a lot of faith in humans.

There was a loud thud in the back of my truck and it caused me to swerve slightly off the road. "Shit!" I yanked on the wheel to correct it.

I glanced into the rear view and through the dark surroundings I could see the outline of a massive *something*, in the bed of my vehicle. Panic ensued and I immediately sped up. The creature looked more than capable of tearing a person apart and flinging their carnage around the woods. I didn't know what it was, but it was thrashing against the window.

I heard glass shatter and could feel claws digging into my shoulder. "Goddamn it!" Slamming my foot down on the brake, I forced the creature's arm from the broken window and sent it rolling over the side of the truck. Quickly, I moved my foot to apply the same pressure on the gas pedal. Speeding off, I found myself watching the shadow disappear further and further down the road.

Fumbling, I reached for my phone while doing my best not to take my eyes off the road. I managed to open contacts and find Griggs. Hitting the call button, it barely rang before he answered. "Hey, Ali. Is everything okay?" He was quick to check in, probably realizing it was unlikely I had made it home already.

"Griggs... there was ...something.... in my truck!" My voice was pitchy and my throat was dry from fear. I glanced down to realize I was driving way too fast, and forced myself to slow down before I hurt someone.

"What? Are you okay?" There was a lot of noise in the background, but I couldn't focus on any one thing or voice.

"I'm okay. It got my arm." I could feel the pain setting in, as the adrenaline lowered slightly the further I drove. The more distance between me and that *thing*, the safer I felt.

"Don't go home. Meet me at the office?" He sounded as panicked as I was.

"Okay." I said simply, knowing I didn't want to hang up, "Just... talk to me while I drive? I need the distraction"

"Of course." There was a slight pause before Griggs started speaking again. "I was just thinking about your book today. The first one you published?"

"You only think about that one because I dedicated it to you." I had to smirk a bit.

"Hey now, that's not true. I'm pretty sure I read most of it!" Griggs chuckled back. "I hope you know I'm real proud of you. I remember you used to think you'd be stuck tagging laundry the rest of your life. You hated that job. You were miserable. Kinda crazy, lookin' at where you are now."

My eyes were filling up with tears as he spoke and I nodded along with his words, "I was. I was terrified to do anything different but didn't want to be stuck in the same. I remember that talk like yesterday."

"I told you you'd find your way. You seem so much happier now. I know the text books drag you down, but the creative bits seem to really make it worth it for you."

"No, they aren't that bad. They definitely feed me and that makes them worth it. It can be weird putting yourself out there with things like what I write. Obviously not the text books."

Griggs scuffled together a laugh. "Right. You deserve that. I'm glad you found something that brings you happiness."

There was still something reassuring about Griggs being on the other end of the line. I didn't hang up with Griggs until I was pulling into the parking lot and could see the building in front of me. I came to an abrupt halt, shaking still, and turned off the truck. Attempting to take a few calming breaths, I slid out of the truck and closed the door.

The parking lot was well-lit, thankfully, and I was able to look at the damage. There was glass in the bed of the truck, just like in the front of it. Scratch marks on the hood led down to the passenger side. I wondered what sort of nails could have shredded metal like this.

I wince as my shoulder was really beginning to pound with pain. Carefully shaking out my clothes, only a few pieces of glass fell out. A majority of it went to the other side of the cab. I knew it would be a few minutes before Griggs was there, but waiting outside wasn't an option.

Deciding it was far better to be inside, I went for the door. A smaller framed female named Lacey smiled up at me. "Oh hi, Ali! Long time no—" her words cut short when she saw the blood on my arm. "What happened?"

Lacey rushed to me and encouraged me to sit. "I'm okay. Just hurts. Something attacked me when I was driving."

Her curiosity was clear across her features but she didn't ask me any other questions. What a sweet girl. I was visibly shaken and it would have been obnoxious to be asked a thousand things that I know I don't have any answers for. "I'll be right back." I watched Lacey leave, assuming she was on her way to get a first aid kit, or some sort of bandaging.

I heard the door open and I jumped a bit at the sound. I was prepared to feel relief that Griggs had made it but instead I was confronted with a stranger's familiar face. "You?" I said out loud, completely against my better judgment.

"John," he said, a small smirk on his face. I stared at him for a long moment before his demeanor shifted when he saw my wound. "Are you okay?"

I glanced down at my wound and dismissed it. "Yeah fine. Are *you* okay?" He had to be there for a reason.

"Yeah, I'm good. I hit some kind of large animal on my way home and it wrecked the front of my car. So I was advised to come do a report."

I watched him as he spoke. His mouth was wide, but not necessarily in a weird way. His eyes were a bright gray, and the difference in our heights felt all the more pronounced with me seated. In his casual attire I could see inked markings on his arms and peeking up over the top of his collar. I couldn't tell what they were, but I was suddenly very aware I was staring.

"I had an incident with an animal on the way home too. Where did you hit it?" I couldn't help but wonder if he had seen the same one I had.

"I live about ten minutes from here, so it was just up the road. I got out to look for it, but I didn't see or hear anything."

Up the road. I felt my eyes grow wide, just as Griggs came stomping into the entrance. He made a beeline for me and pulled me into a hug.

"I'm so glad you're okay." His voice was shaky and he looked terrified. "I looked at your truck...Jesus Christ..." Suddenly he realized there was someone behind him. He glanced over to the total stranger, and John extended his hand.

"Hi, I'm John Belham."

Griggs shook his hand and John looked back at me. "Your truck is messed up too? What was that thing?"

"I don't know. It was big though. And strong." Reliving it was making my heart race again. The thoughts began to spiral with the body I had just seen. I didn't really believe they were connected, strange though they were. They seemed like just a coincidence.

"John?" Lacey called over to him with a big smile that almost made me want to roll my eyes. "Here's some stuff you can fill out. You can come sit right here." She gestured to the other side of her small desk, inviting him closer..

"Uh, okay great. Thanks." John looked Griggs and me over. "You should get that wound looked at. Are you going to be okay?"

I could see the pout on Lacey's lips, and it felt like a weird victory. *Why are we like this?* I wanted to roll my eyes at myself. "Yeah. I'm fine. It hurts, but so does existing." I shrugged, wishing I hadn't said that at all. Isolating yourself from people, turns out, can make you say things that aren't exactly appropriate.

He gave me one more smile and a nod before he went to do the papers for his report. Griggs helped me stand up and move as Lacey was putting out the kit on the counter. "Thanks, Lacey." She smiled and nodded.

Griggs and I stepped into the back office to clean up my arm and stitch it up. The coroner's office was connected to the police station. It sat in a grouping of brick buildings that ranged from DMV to the tax office. Small town living meant all the deemed important buildings were next to each other.

"Whatever got on you, is a damn monster. A goddamn monster!" He was almost choking on his excitement and fear. "I don't know what the hell is going on, but I intend to figure this out."

I remained silent for the time it took him to bandage me. The skin around the wound tingled, almost like feather sensations up and down my right arm. It felt oddly comforting all things considered.

Griggs wasn't a fan of me driving myself home, but with a few cups of mediocre coffee, I was ready to get in some clean clothes and get into my bed. The comfort of home felt too good to ignore the call any longer. "I'll call you in the morning," I told Griggs, hugging him one last time before getting into my truck and heading home.

By the time I woke up my arm was worse. The pain was shooting from my shoulder to my neck and upper back, and then down my arm into my fingers. The blood had soaked through my clothing and my bedding, leaving a large yellow and red mark on everything it touched. It smelled putrid, like decay.

As I tried to get up from my bed, I could feel the fever in my body. My wound was definitely infected. "Fuck," I cursed, trying to find my phone. It was already three in the afternoon.

Seeing Griggs had blown up my messages, I gave him a quick call to update him that my arm was infected, but that I got some sleep. The truth was, I felt like shit.

It took everything in me to tow my ass to the shower. I put on the hot water, plugged the drain, and sluggishly moved to the sink. Trying to process anything I was feeling was overwhelming, to the point tears were falling from my exhausted eyes.

I had slept for over twelve hours and I felt as though I hadn't slept at all. I could feel everything my skin touched and it made my teeth hurt. I fumbled in the cabinet to find something to clean my wound but all I had was some gauze and antibacterial ointment. "It'll do." I said out loud.

The tub was filling up quickly, but I was struggling to move. Caving to the pain, I sunk down to the floor and crawled to the tub. Beyond weak, I managed to get inside and sink into the heat. Using my toes, I cut the water off and let it fall with a 'slap' back into the bath. My wound hurt. A sharp pain was electric through my body as I allowed the water to wash over it.

I hadn't expected the water to turn so murky. The dried blood coming off was changing the water from that pale yellow color all faucet water actually is, to a murky reddish. I realized I should have told Griggs, but the issue was outside of his scope of work. I looked over at the wound and saw the bulging tissue under the stitches he had carefully placed just the night before. It was really bad. I needed to go to a hospital.

Trying to gently wipe off the dried bodily fluids around the wound, the pain only intensified. Watching the infection seemingly pulse beneath the strained stitching, I couldn't help but touch it. I was fascinated by the way this wound functioned. Deep chunks of skin were torn clean out from the claws that hit me. There were small cuts where the tips must have started, then the lines grew quite deep. These markings stretched from the top of my shoulder near my collarbone, and extended down towards my shoulder blade. It took up the entire space. If I took a paper plate and folded it over this area, that was about the size of this swollen gash.

As I traced the wound, intrigued, my head began to pound worse. My vision was blurring. I felt like I was merely a puppet. I simply existed in this battered and exhausted state. My heart was still pounding loudly, as I could feel the vibrations in my chest.

I believed I was going to die from the injury. I cursed myself for being so stubborn. For not going to the hospital the night before.

Accidentally pressing too hard on the wound, a pillowy white substance leaked out the corner and slid down my wet flesh to my fingers. As I played with the texture, the pain in my forehead was so severe I was forced to squint. I watched my fingers slip through the chunky liquid and I wanted to gag. My stomach was flipping and at any moment, I was sure I was going to vomit.

And yet...

I lifted my fingers with the cloudy goo sliding around and put it to my lips. As if controlled by something else, my tongue crept between my parted lips and lapped up the pus like liquid. My body lurched forward and demanded more. Against my own will, my hand scratched and tore at the wound. I scooped up blood, infection, and flesh, greedily shoving it into my mouth. I could barely move seconds before, but this hunger has given me a new motivation.

I didn't stop until the wound was almost down to my bone. The water was a rust color of blood, remains, and sickness. I sighed in contentment, licking my lips for any traces left of the meal I had consumed. I let my hands fall into the tub as I tried to ignore what I had just done. I didn't want to believe it was real. Surely it wasn't real.

My eyes were fluttering slowly, and I could see a shape in the water with me. Someone was on their knees in front of me. I felt the desire to speak, but was unable to do so. I was so weak that I couldn't do *anything*. I couldn't move to protect myself, or scramble to get away. The wound pulsated, the iron taste and bitterness still lingering on my tongue from my meal. Watching with as much energy as I could muster, the shape shifted and turned. Clawed fingers reached out to grasp either side of my tub and as it leaned in it growled a heavy grunt in my face. The skeletal features around the mouth extended and stretched outside of the normal shape of a human face. It brushed my cheek and whispered, 'Indulge.'

I don't remember falling asleep. The freezing water around my body is likely what woke me up. I jumped forward, gasping for air as though my head had been held under water. I was frantically looking around to find the creature that had somehow found my home and crept into my bath. There was no sign of it. It took a moment for me to register that I was fine. I glanced over at the wound and all that remained was a faded, pink mark, outlining a slightly dented space on my shoulder.

My fingers ran over my flesh and I was confused, but also relieved. It didn't make any sense. A wound that infected, that big, would have taken weeks, if not months to heal. I didn't understand what the fuck was going on with me. My headache was gone. My body felt normal. The vision issues I had were completely resolved. The only thing bothering me was how cold I felt in the tub.

With ease, I was able to climb from the tub and dry myself off. I got dressed in something to help warm me up and I went to get something to drink. My throat felt a little raw and irritated, but I couldn't believe how normal I felt otherwise. I needed to call Griggs but didn't know what to tell him. That I dreamt I ate from my wound and now I'm healed? That didn't add up, and I couldn't afford to look like I had completely lost my mind.

As soon as I got settled, my phone was buzzing. The water I consumed helped my throat, so I cleared it and answered. Griggs was a mountain of questions. I could barely keep up.

"I'm fine, actually. A bit tired and sore. The wound is better, though. I'm going to regret sleeping all day when I sit down to do some work later." There was a pause.

"Why don't I bring you dinner?" His tone was one I knew better than to argue with.

"Fine. Oh, I wanted to ask you," I shifted in my bed to get comfortable again, "did they find out who was in the woods yet?"

The hesitation was long but there was noise in the background so I dismissed it, "Yeah, we'll talk when I get there. It is a little chaotic here today."

Even though I wanted some answers, I didn't want to push. "What about John? Did he file the report for his car?" Maybe I needed the comfort of Griggs on the phone more than I realized. I felt reluctant to let him off the line.

"John? Oh, the guy that hit something. I think so. He was talking with someone before you left, but I'm on the wrong side of things to follow up. I did tell one of the detectives from last night that the creature he hit, the one you were attacked by, could be what we're looking for what happened in the woods."

"I really wanted to talk to him to find out what he saw, but I guess it didn't seem like the time." I rotated my shoulder on autopilot, expecting it to hurt and surprised when it didn't.

"I can see if they got anywhere with it. I'll pack up here and bring something over. Pizza okay?"

"Yeah, pizza is fine." My mouth salivated and my stomach clenched up in agreement, "Oh Griggs," I paused, "can you make it Meat Lovers?"

I must have dozed off again, because I woke up to loud bangs on my door. "Shi" I rolled off the bed and headed to the door.

"What the hell, Ali?" Griggs looked panicked, "I've been here banging for fifteen minutes. I was about to break a window."

"In my defense, I was just horribly mangled by a beast seeing a body torn to shreds in the woods *and* I had a lot of blood loss. I'm fucking tired."

His features softened and he sighed. "I know. I'm sorry. This whole thing has me on edge, and I'm worried we're gonna find more bodies. Blood loss is why I was so worried. I brought the food." He showed me the box, and I moved back so he could come in.

Getting settled in the living room, I took a slice and began chowing down as I sat on my feet on the sofa. "Thank you. You're a saint." I spoke through a mouthful of food.

"I need to talk to you about something. It was why I wanted to come over."

I looked up. "That sounds...serious."

"We did get the results back on the body in the woods." I set my food down and stared at him. "There's just no easy way to say this."

"It was Althea?" I was leaning forward in my seat, my eyes filling with tears that had been vacant at her wake.

I could see Griggs visibly swallow the feelings he had. "Yes."

"That can't be right. She was embalmed. We saw her in the casket at the service." It felt like a natural place to start. The last logical thing I could wrap my brain around before it turned into utter confusion.

"I know. I can't make it make sense either. I... I wish I knew. The way the remains were, there's no way that she was embalmed." His hands were rubbing together frantically.

The pizza felt like a rock in the pit of my stomach. "I'm gonna be sick." I covered my mouth and unfolded myself from sitting to rush to the bathroom. Crumpling to the floor on my knees, I wretched into the toilet. The pizza emptied, and all my confusion and disgust came up with it. Nothing made any fucking sense.

I threw up until my vision was blurred. All the energy I had before was depleted. Griggs didn't interrupt. Smart move. I would have bitten his head off. Rinsing my mouth out and washing my hands, I came out of the bathroom and stood, staring at him.

"I don't have any answers." He offered. "What can I do to help?"

I shook my head. Nothing. There was nothing he could do. There was nothing anyone could do. I needed to understand how this could happen. Who was responsible. How a body that was supposed to be embalmed and buried ended up torn to pieces in a bloody mess in the middle of the woods.

"I wasn't even close to her. I sat at her wake feeling nothing, just waiting for it to be over. Now..."

There was a soft sigh from Griggs. "Don't let yourself fall into that trap. It's perfectly normal to be respectful, but not necessarily be sad.."

I forced myself to come sit back down, but I couldn't stop chewing on my nails. "Does my mom know?"

"I won't know that until later. But safe to say, if she hasn't called you, she probably doesn't know. I wouldn't blame them for putting it off." There was a heavy moment of silence. "It's a hard thing to explain." ."

"This feels wrong, Griggs. This whole situation. The body going missing. Being torn apart. The attack on my truck. Another guy hitting something with his car. What is happening here?"

The silence around us was all encompassing. "I was really hoping you'd know. I know I don't always take what you do seriously, but I respect you for what you work on. This really feels like something... else. I mean, the only theory I've got right now is a monster from one of your books."

"It could have been someone from the funeral home. But we've known those people forever. It would be hard to imagine them..." but that was a joke. I knew better than to think of something like that. People couldn't be trusted. It was always the ones you thought you knew. That was why I kept myself in my books and out of the real world.

"Uh, Ali?" I stopped my own maddening spiral of thoughts and looked to Griggs who was staring at me in disbelief. At the wound, or lack thereof, which I had entirely forgotten to cover up.

"Look, I know it is weird... I'm guessing it just wasn't as bad as we thought it was?" I tried weakly to deflect, but it didn't work.

"I saw how deep that wound was. The stitches were necessary because of the depth. How is it just... gone?"

I continued to avoid his gaze, contemplating picking up food again but deciding against it. My stomach wanted more, but I was worried I'd just throw it up again. I could have pretended to have answers, but I didn't see the point. There was a lot of really weird shit going on, but my injury didn't give me any more answers than Griggs had.

We sat in silence again, this time for a while. No matter how many slices I ended up trying to eat, my stomach grumbled with urgency for more. I felt like I was starving. The center of my stomach felt like a black hole.

My body had been through so much, it wasn't unreasonable to expect things would be off. Maybe it wasn't hunger. I thought back to the tub, and was surprised to find I wasn't repulsed at the memory.

"Ali?" Griggs' voice pulled me back into the moment and I sighed.

"I'm so out of it. Been a long few days. So did you talk to my mom?"

"I spoke to her late yesterday but it wasn't a very productive conversation." He looked defeated.

"Sounds about right. I wish I had taken it more seriously when she told me about the body missing. I dismissed her as a crazy woman. Even though I knew it wasn't just a normal thing. I feel pretty shitty to be honest."

Griggs stood, picking up the empty box. "Don't. Who knows how to handle those conversations anyway?"

I decided to follow him into the kitchen to throw away the pizza container. "I know, but still."

He turned to me then, with genuine concern in his eyes. "Maybe you should take it easy for another day before jumping back into reality. I'm not sure what to make of any of this, but I sure hope you don't find yourself turning at the next full moon."

The humor didn't land for either of us. I was worried about my condition, and so was he. "Right." I tried to not sound as awkward as I felt.

My stomach was flipping again. Begging me for something else to eat. The pizza had been remarkably delicious for a takeaway. It still hadn't been enough. The taste was fulfilling to my senses, but not to my stomach.

Leaning in as Griggs went to hug me goodbye, I could see that figure again. The one from the tub. I could see it crystal clear, standing right behind us. I didn't react though. I stared at it. Horns extending out both sides of the skeletal face.

It towered over us, bending on bony knees. Parts of its body were covered in thick fur, other parts covered in tissue and muscle. Long, thick claws scratched into my kitchen flooring. Perhaps the most captivating feature was its eyes. They were hollowed out, but with a small, glowing orb in the dead center of each socket. They called to me. Told me to indulge. Encouraged me to be hungry no more.

As Griggs leaned back to leave, my face buried into his neck. My teeth, somehow sharp enough, tore into his flesh and my body hunched into his to knock him to the ground. He cried out, fighting me, and yanking at my clothing to get me off of him. I couldn't stop.

Bite after bite.

I yanked flesh from his body. His strength was useless against my own. I was devouring him so quickly, I couldn't even process what I was doing. Blood and skin covered my face and my nails were digging into him to hold him still. I was chewing through his limbs until they fell away from his body. His chest was wide open with wounds. Eventually, he stopped moving.

All at once the hunger ceased. I was overly full and certain I was going to throw up. Only I didn't. Instead, I snapped my head back with a loud gasping sound as blood oozed down my face, neck, and arms. What was left of the body beneath me was unrecognizable.

The realization of what I had done slammed into me. I scrambled backwards on all fours until my back hit my kitchen wall. Tears poured down my face, likely making streaks through the blood that had already started to dry on my skin.

I could feel that my mouth was open, but I was sobbing so hard that no sound came out. My entire body was shaking. I was completely at a loss. I just murdered one of the only people I had in my life that I cared about.

The creature was gone, but I was unsure for how long. I stood frozen in that spot for a long time. My body hurt, but I was no longer hungry. I could hear the thoughts in my head smacking against my barely conscious state. 'You'll get used to it.'

I finally made myself stand up.

I made myself go to my phone.

I made myself call 9-1-1.

I made myself lie.

I compelled myself to fuck up my front door and make drag marks from the door to the kitchen where Griggs laid completely in pieces. I forced myself to tear into my shoulder as best as I could. I couldn't quite reach the exact spot of the wound, but I couldn't be unscathed. I bit myself over and over until I felt it was believable. Then, I cleaned up enough so that it wasn't on my face.

I could hear the sirens and my heart shattered. I knew I had to to lie to these people and tell them we were attacked. I had to make it seem like the same animal as before. These people knew me, and they knew my close relationship with Griggs. It had to make sense. If I failed, I knew that I would be locked up. I knew also, that I deserved far worse.

The ambulance arrived with a police vehicle right behind it. No one could believe what they were looking at. I had a dismembered body in my lap. I was stroking Griggs' bloody face. My body was hunched over him and I couldn't stop crying to even talk to them. I didn't have to fake that part. They asked me what happened, I told them about my own attack, and it seemed fine. They bought it. They comforted me. They asked me if I had somewhere else to stay. I told them no. They offered to help clean up as they took the body and the pieces that were no longer attached.

The whole ordeal took hours. My body felt amazing, energized. My emotions, however, were completely unstable and broken. I had no one. I was dealing with this completely alone. I had taken a life, an important life to me, and I still didn't understand why.

I found myself sitting in bed and staring at nothing in particular. It was the next afternoon, but I hadn't t slept at all. My mom has called several times, no doubt having heard of the body in the woods. I couldn't handle that conversation at that moment, and decided to text her that I wasn't not feeling well instead. I knew if I didn't send her something, she would have showed up. I couldn't stomach the thought of what happened to Griggs happening to her.

I searched a few things, when I felt up to it. I tried to find answers, but had zero luck. The hunger began building again, and that time I could feel it starting. My body tensed, as if waiting for me to provide another meal. In the movies, people who desire eating other human beings, usually subside such feelings by eating raw meat. I didn't have any, so it would mean going out in public.

I didn't think I could withstand being in a public place. I didn't want to think about what would happen if I lost control. It wasn't me who took Griggs' life, it was whatever I was turning into. There was a true separation in the two, but that wasn't something I could explain if anyone were to witness me ripping out someone's jugular. As the sensation built I realized it would be better to risk it, rather than waiting until the hunger became insatiable.

Dressing comfortably, I willed myself to get into the car and go to the grocer. I lived in a relatively small town, so I'm sure everyone had heard about the animal attack at my house. They just didn't know *I* was the animal. With my sunglasses still on, I quickly went to the back of the store to find something to ease the pain in my stomach.

I tried to think about anything else. I tried to focus on childhood memories. I tried to think about the plot to my favorite television show. Nothing was working. My stomach growled, and my mouth went dry. I had to be quick. So I grabbed a few steaks and some hamburger meat. Even a pound of bacon. Something had to help right?

I made it through the entire store without a single interaction until I went to cash out. Tossing up the meat, I just wanted to be done. I wanted to get home where it was safe.

"Oh, hi Ali," the girl at the register said. Her name was Tiffany and we had gone to high school together. Her tone was one of sadness. "I'm so sorry about Griggs. How awful to have to see that. Are you doing okay?"

Fumbling with my wallet, I tried not to look too antsy, "I'm okay. I really, I really don't want to talk about it, Tiff. Thank you for the kindness, though. It means a lot." It didn't. But she didn't need to know that.

I might be a cynic, but I'm not an asshole. She had never been cruel to me and there was no reason to be cruel to her. Paying for the meat, I felt like my feet couldn't carry me fast enough. Exiting the store, I glanced down to shove my receipt in one of the bags and collided into another human.

"Shit, I'm sorry." I looked up and locked eyes with John. He smiled immediately, and I felt my skin vibrate. *What the fuck?*

"No problem. You okay?" He sounded genuinely worried, but I couldn't tell why exactly.

We were in a small town, that was true. But I had never seen John until Althea's funeral. It made me wonder who he was here for. Did he live here now? Why was he lingering? My head was racing and I hated how chaotic everything about my life felt in that moment.

"Yeah, fine," I answered. He eyed my bags and I stepped around him. "Well, see ya around."

He turned to face me as I started to move towards my vehicle. "Hey, wait." My entire body stopped and I was frozen in place. It was like a trance, only it felt so natural. "I know there's a lot going on. Would you be open to letting me come keep you company tomorrow? We can go for a walk, or get some lunch?"

I was awestruck. Any other time in my life, I would have been excited and giddy. He was incredibly good looking, and he seemed nice. I didn't think, however, that I was in a position to be meeting up with someone only two days after eating a man who was like family to me. The idea made my stomach flip, but I had to admit that right now the hunger felt calmer. I didn't feel the urgency to eat that I had only moments ago.

I looked back up at John. "I don't really think now is the—" but I was cut off.

"I'll just come by tomorrow. If you decide then you don't want to see me, I'll leave it alone. I just think you could benefit from a friend right now."

I didn't say much else as he turned and walked inside the store. I was angry. I felt confused. I didn't have any fucking answers and I wasn't any closer to figuring out my problem. It was the way he said it. He had disregarded my refusal to make the decision for me and I didn't like that. He was going to be in for a rude awakening.

Getting home with the meat, I started to put everything away, minus one pack of hamburger. It seemed like a good enough starting point and this was what I had seen done in the media. If this didn't work, I wasn't sure what the next steps would be. I couldn't continue killing people.

Opening the packaging, I took a few deep breaths. The smell was intriguing and it made my stomach growl louder. I gripped the side of the counter and stepped back, letting my head fall down as I tried to just act and not think. Standing up, I quickly dug my hand into the meat and scooped it into my mouth. The greasy, cold texture made my body convulse, but my tongue wasn't angry. It took more energy than I thought it would to finish it. I gagged a few times, the smell of the raw meat not as appealing as people apparently.

I sludged my way down onto the floor and pulled my knees up to my chest. The hunger was worse. The raw meat didn't help. I didn't want to cave to the emotions, but I couldn't control them. I began to shake from the tears, sobbing uncontrollably on the kitchen floor. There was a weird residue left on my lips and it made me gag again. My stomach emptied right next to me on the floor. Chunks of raw meat, bile, and blood spilled out of me like a fountain. I could feel the burning in my nose from it and my throat constricted around the hunks of beef that were not good enough for my stomach.

I sat there snotty, covered in spit and vomit. My nose, throat, and mouth burned. I didn't have it in me to stand yet, but I knew I couldn't just sit there in a pile of my own sick. Weakly, I reached up to the counter to pull myself up. I turned on the faucet, splashed my face and drank from the sink. Swishing it around and spitting out the leftover chunks from my teeth.

"What the fuck am I gonna do?" My words were hoarse from the violent episode.

It took me an hour to get the mess cleaned up. I took a shower and climbed back into my bed. It was incredibly difficult to sleep through the hunger. It settled a bit by nightfall, but that didn't mean I got any sleep. I tossed and turned most of the night with visions of that creature. Realizing that I couldn't trust myself around humans, I didn't know how I was supposed to get help.

Rolling around in my bed, I was covered in sweat, and in more pain than a human being should ever suffer. My stomach was cramping, and my abdomen and lower back were also clenched up in pain. I knew then that it wouldn't just go away. The realization made me feel defeated. Like I had lost. I wasn't safe. Not for others and not for myself. My shoulder was aching again and I just wanted it all to stop. I couldn't do it anymore.

I could hear a knocking at my door, and I couldn't have cared less who it was. I wasn't in a space for company, and no one was safe around me. It was best to pretend not to be home. To pretend I was dead. Which I wanted to be. I didn't have anything worth sticking around for anyway. My mom would hurt, but she'd heal. Griggs was gone. I had no relationship. I had no kids. I had no other friends. I didn't even have a following for my books. What difference would it even make?

The knocking ceased, but I heard my front door open. *Shit.* My mom had a spare key. I couldn't do it. If she walked into the room I'd hurt her.

I'd kill her.

"Mom, please do not come in here! I need you to go. It isn't sa—" my words got stuck in my throat as I faced the door and saw John standing in it. "Wh—you? You need to..." but my stomach locked up again and I rolled into a ball so fast, I fell off my bed and onto the floor.

John came over and reached for me and I tried to push him away. I knew something was off about him. He had just broken into my house. I didn't know how, or for what reason. I could hardly move away from him. So I was forced to stay put, lingering in this unsafe situation. My mind started to wander. If I needed to eat, and he broke into my house, the problem could essentially take care of itself.

This time when he offered a hand to help, I decided to try and take a bite. I lunged forward but I couldn't follow through. He smelt off. Like death and rot. My nose scrunched, but my stomach relaxed a bit.

"Let me help you, Ali." His voice was soft and kind, but I wasn't buying it.

"H-h-h-how did you know where I lived?" I pushed my body back and bumped into my side table. I was terrified, but in so much pain. I wasn't sure what I had the bandwidth to focus on first. The idea of attacking him felt repulsive and I was left even more confused than before.

"I know you're going through a lot. You really should let me help you." Surprisingly, he backed away, leaning against the wall near the door to my bedroom.

"I'm really sick. You need to stay away from me." I lurched into my words, as if I had to physically move to make them come out.

"I know. That's why I'm here." I didn't like the way that sounded.

"What's.... your connection?" I had weird suspicions seeing him here, and now I knew he was connected to whatever was happening in the town.

"You need to eat first. You won't be up for listening to me much while you're in that much pain." He stepped closer, and I flinched.

"I'm fine." I stated, processing a little late that he knew what I was feeling.

"Trust me, you're not. If you keep ignoring it, you're going to go into a craze. That isn't something you can just come back from." John left the room, and I tried to look around for something I could use as a weapon.

He sounded too sure of himself. He knew this feeling, and he knew the risks. My energy was lacking, and by the time he returned, I hadn't managed to moved a muscle. There was a package in his hand, wrapped in brown paper. My stomach growled loudly, and my mouth salivated. I crawled forward on hands and knees and yanked the package from his hands. Barely able to get the paper off, I was tearing into the meat like the savage I had become.

John wasn't surprised by the sight, and he had known exactly what to get me. This wasn't like the hamburger meat I tried earlier. Within minutes I was done and my pains were easing. I could focus again, and once again I felt strong. I felt okay.

Standing up, I used my sweatshirt sleeve to wipe my mouth and I glared at him. "Explain. Now."

John smirked, but put his hands up and nodded. "Okay." He sat on the floor, crossing his legs. "You should sit though."

I didn't want to listen, but I knew whatever he was about to say was going to be bizarre. So I did as he suggested.

"I didn't know anyone at the funeral." The thought had already occurred to me, but I didn't say anything. "I went to interact with you."

I felt sick to my stomach. What kind of weird stalker situation had I found myself in? "Why me?" I managed. He had a lot to explain, and flying off the handle wasn't going to get me answers any quicker.

"You know that emptiness you feel? That primal sense of loneliness? When it is more than just wanting company or someone to sleep with? Real, honest emptiness?"

My eyes watered at the question and I hated how easy it was to nod my head.

"Me too. When this came to me, I was the exact same as you. I found projects to occupy my mind, but there was nothing any human being could offer me that would cure the hunger I had to feel like a part of something. To feel, really feel, anything..." he trailed off, and his eyes drifted from mine for only a moment. "I felt that same feeling from you. This was meant to be a rest stop for me, but I could almost taste your loneliness. I could smell the depth of your emptiness."

"Fast forward." I demanded, feeling sicker the more he spoke about me and what he *felt*.

"So I met you. I was planning on leaving town, but I wasn't careful. I went too long in the presence of people and so..." He swallowed hard, and I closed my eyes. "I... interfered. I didn't mean for things to happen this way. But I was there the night you went to the woods. I was watching and waiting. I wanted an opportunity to-"

"To turn me into a fucking monster?" His brow raised, clearly surprised how even toned I remained.

"You don't have to look at it that way. This thing inside me feeds on the feeling of hunger. No matter what it is someone might hunger for. I wasn't in control the night I attacked you."

I knew it was him now, but hearing it conjured such a strange slew of emotions. The air in my lungs felt cold. I felt depleted of any energy to care. Something in me clawed beneath the surface, and I knew that this really wasn't any different than how I was living my life before. Except for back then, I wasn't slaughtering my loved ones.

"That was why I followed you to the station, to see if you were okay. I have never done this before. The intense feelings you have right now will ease. You'll learn to have a schedule, and it'll get easier."

I scoffed. "So I'm what? Stuck as a cannibal now? I wish you had just killed me that night." I brought my knees up to my face and rested my head on them.

"I'm sorry. I know it doesn't seem fair, but we met for a reason."

That triggered a rage inside me. "We didn't meet! You stalked me, and inserted yourself into my life. Pretended to be someone visiting. To be someone that might be trustworthy. It was all a lie. A lie for what? So you could force me to live some fucked up monster lover daydream of yours? If you were that lonely you could have left me the fuck out of it!" My hands were knotted in each other.

"Ali..." I shot him a glare that made him stop and think about his next sentiment. "I can still help you. I can help you learn to deal with this, so you don't hurt anyone you care about. There's ways."

"Please leave." I was crying again, and I hated it. I hated that he was invoking all these things in me. Why was I even so disappointed? I didn't know him. I had zero reasons to carry expectations.

He said he wasn't in control, and *that* I understood. I truly was no better having murdered someone I cared about only two days prior. Griggs' blood was on John's hands too. He was to blame for all of this.

"If I leave, you'll hurt more people without guidance. I don't expect forgiveness, not yet. But I can help keep things under control, and I can help get you acclimated." He was still speaking so normally, so calmly. He of course knew I wouldn't have much of a choice.

"And why can't I just end this myself? I don't want to learn to just accept it." I was able to find enough strength to keep my voice stable this time.

"You mean die? You already did. The night in the bathtub. When you woke up renewed?"

I had no words for how angry this made me. "So you *were* there?" I stood then, pacing and chewing on my thumbnail.

"Not in that way, no. We're connected, though. So I could see things as you saw them for a bit. Just before you came to."

I put my hands to my temple and stopped moving. Huffing, I tried to calm my thoughts into useful questions. "I died?"

John was quiet long enough, it made me look at him again. "Technically, yes."

"So this is like a vampire thing? Or... a zombie?" The question felt stupid, but once again I was not getting answers fast enough.

I could tell it was hard for John not to laugh, but he stifled his humor and cleared his throat again. "No. Nothing like that. This is more of a spiritual thing, I think."

"You *think*?"

"Look, I haven't been this way forever. It happened to me in a different way than it happened to you. I'm still learning. It seems to be a process. You're still you, but that will change. The entity inside will make your body into its own. Shifting and changing it into the creature I know you've been seeing. I saw it too. Then I became it. But it takes time."

I wasn't prepared to hear that this wasn't over. That there was more to come. So I said nothing. I sat back down on my bed and stared at the carpet. I thought about what my life had become. And the only person who could help me, was the one who put me here in the first place. I had seen this play out a thousand times in media, but this wasn't supposed to be real life. If I thought I had it in me, I'd just kill him. Although he had hinted such a thing would not be possible.

"So that's that. I get no say. I can't even end it if I want to. I'm just stuck like this." John didn't seem as relaxed before. I could tell he knew this feeling well.

"I know it holds no weight now, but I am sorry. I couldn't ignore the call, and I didn't mean to attack you. I've never done that before." So he had already said. It wouldn't matter how many times I heard it, I could never forgive him.

My life was far from perfect, but it was *mine*. I had control. I had a say in how it was. I chose to live it this way and now I had to find ways to unlearn my habits and tendencies. I had to learn how to not hurt other people. People who, before today, I hadn't given a fuck about. Now I wanted to save them all. A little too late for that perspective.

If I refused his help, I'd be on my own navigating something I didn't understand. If I tried to run, I'd end up in the same situation. In truth, I wasn't scared of John. The feelings I carried were just anger and disdain. Feelings I was, at this point, used to feeling. I felt myself sink further into the bed the longer I sat.

"I think I just want you to leave." I didn't look up as I spoke. "I know I don't have any real choice in what the next few months or years look like, but right now I can control this. And I don't want to look at you."

John stood, which I only knew because it was followed by the sounds of him moving further away. "I understand."

"You couldn't possibly understand." There was silence as he stood there. I could still *feel* him standing there. "When I'm ready to learn, you'll know. But for right now, stay away from me."

I forced myself up to lead him to the door. Something in me needed to make sure he left. He had come in and made himself at home in my body and in my home. Enough was enough. Opening the door I followed him out onto the front stoop as he stopped walking and turned to face me.

"You should probably find a way to accept this sooner or later."

I was gritting my teeth as I stared at him. "You don't get to decide that." My fists were clenched at my sides. My voice louder than I meant for it to be.

"I'm not trying to decide." He stepped closer and I retreated a bit. "If you don't find a way to figure out your hunger, you'll hurt someone you care about. Your mom? Someone innocent from town?"

My anger was bubbling. I could feel the rage bile building in my throat. Stomping closer to him, I began yelling. "And whose fault do you think that would be? Huh? Certainly not the girl who was just driving home one night. Certainly not the woman who has lived a quiet and reclusive life. Certainly not an innocent human being that *you* took advantage of!"

John's expressions didn't falter. "You should calm down..." he kept his eyes on mine and all it did was push me further.

"Or what?" I shoved him backwards, the strength from the meal making him at least stumble back a bit. "You'll kill me? Hurt me? Leave me? You've already done the worst possible fucking thing you could have done!" I shoved him again.

There was a moment where he looked like he was contemplating walking away. Instead, he planted himself, and watched me. The confidence enraged me and I reared my right fist back and slammed against that smug jawline. My fingers felt like they had snapped in half. I called out in pain and tried to shake it off. Looking back up to see if I had accomplished anything, John's eyes glowed and his mouth shifted and cracked as it was set.

I realized in slow, horror, that I had knocked his jaw out of place. He snapped his teeth at me and growled. There was a moment of panic, and for a split second I almost ran.

I reminded myself that whatever monstrous strength he was displaying, he had given to me as well.

So I didn't run.

I hit him again.

And again.

The last time I tried, John caught my wrist and threw me to the ground. He had barely moved but I was on my back in seconds. Rolling over, I stood up quickly and watched in horror as John's flesh fell from his body and was replaced with bone and mats of hair. Large, eight point antlers grew from his skull and he rotated his neck as his long arms hung down low connecting to large, extremely sharp talons.

I felt my mouth hang open as I watched him shift from the seemingly harmless man, to this monster I had only seen faded versions of in my mind. I felt a lump in my throat and my eyes watered. Taking a few steps back, I was afraid to blink. He had been this *thing,* a lot longer than I had been.

John charged me. Galloping hard and fast in my direction, I could think of nothing to do but run. I didn't know how to do that. I wasn't that strong. He was on me too fast, knocking me over and knocking his skeletal mouth against my head. The hit was hard and I felt dizzy from it. He screeched down at me, in a display of dominance.

Kicking my legs up, I tried to keep him from staying too close. My hands shoved upwards hard and I felt warmth on my fingertips. No, not my fingertips. I had shoved my hands into his chest and at the end, as I pulled them down, were the same large and extremely sharp talons. My body jerked and I felt pain in my ribs. There were small wounds from my claws in his chest and blood seeped forward.

It didn't deter him from trying to pin me. Reaching up towards his face, I gripped the bottom of the skeletal mouth and forced it upwards. Pushing John back as hard as I could, I managed to get him off so that I could stand up. The claws had already gone away and I found myself missing them. I felt defenseless. He must have realized it because he was advancing again.

Going inside didn't seem like a good idea, so I ran to the side of the house. I had a few gardening things that might be sharp enough to do some damage. I had to try. The anger still coursing through my veins, I found the energy to move quickly. It took no time for John to catch up to me and for me to realize there was nothing big enough to do anything. I was breathing heavily and my head was spinning. I couldn't think of how to react fast enough.

In one swipe of his claws, I felt them dig into my flesh on my face as I was tossed to the side. Effortlessly. Again. Immediately the blood ran down my face and onto my neck. I could feel the searing pain and it wasn't enough to stop me from being just angry. The fear left my body and my head bumped against the coiled up hose connected to the side of my house.

Clumsy fingers moved over the scaly texture of the hose. John moved closer to me, a monstrous claw raised to strike me again. Slinging the hose upward, it hit him in the face and fell flat beside me. I tried again and this time he caught it, yanking it from my hand and tossing it back beside me. I couldn't be sure, but I swear it sounded like he was laughing at me.

The ground felt wet and cold beneath me as I struggled to back away from his towering form. John was so close I could smell him. He smelled repulsive. The mix of earth and death invaded my senses and I felt like I could gag. Pressing one large talon into my chest, I screamed out in pain. I grasped his leathery wrist to try and prevent it from pushing straight through me.

I could feel my body stiffening beneath the weight he was forcing down on my chest. Tears slipped out of the corners of my eyes and my mouth remained open in a cacophony of pain and defeat. I wondered if he was going to kill me. I wondered if he was even in control at that moment.

I turned my head away, not wanting to look at him any longer if it was the end for me. My eyes fell once more on the hose and although I was certain it was a horrible idea, I had to try again. With one swift thrust against his leg, my strength was enough to knock him off of me. All the while his claws shredded my chest, shoulder and arm, in doing so.

Rolling onto my side, I snatched the hose again and tossed it up, this time catching over his head. I knew it wouldn't stay, he was already moving to put me back on the ground. It was excruciating to move, but I was running on pure adrenaline at this point. Catching the other end of the hose, I yanked it down and grabbed the other side with my slightly less wounded hand. Forcefully pulling down, I was able to snatch John's neck down and he became a little less stable until he finally fell down. Climbing on top of his massive back, I continued pulling. He scratched at me and thrust his body around wildly to try and get me off; he failed.

As I sat on top of this monster I was set to become, I could picture that body in pieces in the wood. I remembered the way he smiled at me, and was kind to me at the funeral. A burning sort of emotion settled into my belly and I pulled.

I thought about growing up with a mother who felt absent and a father that had moved on with his life when I was still in grade school. I could feel the pain of losing Griggs, and the realization I'd never allow myself any reprieve from the guilt.

I pulled.

I could feel my legs getting shaky from blood loss, but I persevered. I could remember the pain and fear I felt when this creature landed on my truck and inflicted a wound that would change my life forever. I could see myself devouring my wound and seeing the cloudy visions of what was to come. Nothing could have ever prepared me for this. Nothing.

I pulled.

I pulled until I heard a large, resounding *crack*. John went limp beneath me and he no longer attempted to knock me off. When I glanced down at the hose, there was blood and gore all over the neck of the beast. I had pulled it almost completely through his throat. My tears felt cold as they rushed down my face and I felt like my body was going to give into the pain from my wounds.

My head hurt, my body ached, and I felt... *better*.

I climbed off John's back and slowly moved towards the front of my house. I felt like I had really achieved something. I hadn't been able to save myself or get rid of the monster inside of me but at least I felt strong and vindicated.

I stepped into my home and realized I was left as I had wanted to be; alone. Left with these feelings and questions. Left with a hunger that was satisfied for now, but would be back soon with a vengeance. Whatever my future held, I was stuck in this new reality. I didn't know where to start unpacking all of this but I decided a good place might be to let my body feel what he wanted to feel. So I did.

For the first time in my adult life, I just let myself feel. All of the anger and confusion, all the pain and the sadness, it all washed over me and I let myself crumble. I allowed myself to completely fall apart. There was nothing to hold back anymore. I cried until my body hurt. My eyes were on fire and my tear ducts expended. The only thing that remained was a calm sense of acceptance. Acceptance that this wouldn't be the last time I felt this way. Acceptance that my life, as I knew it, was over. Acceptance that I was a monster. Acceptance I was going to hurt more people. And then a weird fleeting thought.

Maybe this was exactly what I needed after all.

After I was able to catch my breath again, I knew it was time to go see what to do about this monstrous body in my yard. Surrounded by woods, I could try and dispose of it. I could turn it into the proper authorities, but I didn't like what that could mean for me. My shoulder was healing but it seemed like the deep scratches in my chest were going to take time. I'd likely have to find something to eat to make it heal any faster; that had been the pattern.

Still covered in blood and dirt, I went out to my stoop and took a deep breath. Outside just smelled so normal. A feeling I greatly missed. Rounding the corner to my house, I felt my knees weaken and buckle. Losing my footing, I leaned against the side of the house for support. Red and guts were all over the ground. My hose is a torn mess at this point. But in the center of it all, inside the outline of the fight that had just taken place, was nothing.

No human John.

No creature.

Nothing.

I was left as I had wanted to be; alone. Of all the emotions I was feeling, comforted was not one of them.

A CHANGE IN YOU

There was a lot of pain and reconciliation ahead of Julia Maeve. As she pulled into a gas station near Hayton Town, she was starting to feel nervous. It was time to patch things with Peter. To tell him everything that had happened in their time apart, and to be honest with her journey and where she needed to go. Hayton was a place she had mixed feelings about, but the longer she and Peter were together, the better she felt about being there.

Her car's light had come on just a few miles before, and it was better to stop now then possibly not make it into the small town. There were neighboring spots, but she didn't know them that well. It was too risky knowing there was still something very dark in the town her lover was so connected to.

The station only had two pumping stations and she noticed right away the lack of card readers. "Shit," she said out loud. Knowing she didn't have any cash, all she could see was the dimly lit ATM machine on the side of the building. It was still early in the evening, but it had already started to get dark.

Of course you have to go to the scary ATM in a weird ass town in nowheresville. Rolling her eyes at her current horror movie status, she made her way over to the machine. Card at the ready, she just needed to pay the ridiculous fee and collect enough to get her to Hayton. The rest would be fine. She had been through a lot, but there were still plenty of things to fear in the dark.

The wind moved around the side of the building, creating a funneled sound of chaos and branches cracking. A shiver ran down her spine, and she had the distinct feeling she was being watched. There was something in the air she couldn't quite place. Looking around, she didn't see anyone. The tenant inside could not be seen through the thick, dark glass on the windows. *Get it together Jules.*

Pushing her card into the machine, it beeped loudly. Punching in her pin, it felt like an eternity before it finally came up with the options she needed to withdraw cash. Pressing the **NO RECEIPT** button, she shook her leg in her stance. "Come on. Come on." She could still feel the eyes, and something told her to hurry up.

The cash came out, and the wind caught it right as it was coming out of the machine. "Oh no you don't," Julia muttered, snatching the bills before they could drag her away into the dark of the trees around her. Feeling like she had just avoided at least one easy death in a movie, she tugged on the door to go inside. A little bell rang but there was no one to be found.

"Hello?" she called out, but there was no answer. Going over to the drinks, she opened a door and grabbed a bottle of water. It felt warm in her hand, and she grimaced. One of the circular mirror detection devices in the corner of where she stood reflected movement from behind her.

Julia jumped and turned to face that direction, but she didn't see anything. *Time to go.* She told herself. Going over to the counter, she leaned over to see if she could see anyone in the backroom that connected. No one was there and she sighed. "Hello? I just need to pay for my water and some gas?"

Frustration slowly turned into panic. The longer she was in that dingy store, the more unsettled she felt. There was a rustling from behind the counter and she frowned. Almost picturing a half deaf older man who very likely hated his job, she decided it would be okay to just go look and see. Rounding the corner, she could see a door in the back was wide open. Maybe someone was taking out the trash?

Stepping around further, her boot slid, and she glanced down. In dark crimson contrast to the yellow crusted floor, Julia saw who she assumed to be the cashier. The Middle was torn out and half of his arm was missing. Swallowing hard, Julia's eyes filled with tears. Terrified, she reached the counter and turned in a hurry to flee the building. Sliding in the blood, her boot still soaked, she immediately fell forward and crashed in a magazine rack full of older news articles and Hustlers.

A low, guttural growl came from in front of her and rounding one of the aisles in the small store was a bulky, gray wolf. That wasn't her Peter. That much she knew. Eyeing her exit, the monster's shoulders went back and she tried to breathe. Before allowing it a chance to launch, she picked up the rack and tossed it at the wolf before scrambling behind the counter. Dropping her water and money all in one effortless 'fuck it' of a run.

The wolf was on her, though. It lunged across the side of the counter and Julia threw herself over the front before landing back on the floor. Right then, her goal was to keep distance between them. That was all she could do until trying to exit the store. To her right was the exit, and down a ways in front of her was a door marked **EMPLOYEES ONLY.** Urgently, she moved towards the exit, but the wolf beat her there, causing her to almost collide with its massive frame.

A small yelp escaped Jules as she headed for the door that likely led to a janitor closet. Throwing herself inside, she yanked the door closed. The wolf's claws smacked hard against the door and caused the entire frame to shake. It wouldn't hold forever. What exactly was her plan here?

There was a bell sound from somewhere else in the store and Julia immediately realized it was probably another customer. *Fuck.* The wolf scattered away, and there was quite a bit of commotion in the front. *Now or never, Jules.* Julia pushed out of the door, the wood splintered all over the floor from the power behind the wolf's claws. Carefully, and quietly, she moved closer and closer to the exit. From the mirrors on the corners, she could tell the undeserving patron was being torn to pieces only a few aisles from the door.

The moment her hand pushed on the door, the bell rang again. The same growl as before caused all the hair on her arms to stand up. *Now or never,* she reminded herself as she sprinted out of the store and headed towards her car. She was almost there when she felt teeth sink into her ankle and yank her down onto the cold, busted up gravel of the parking lot.

With the breath knocked out of her, she clutched at the crumbling rocks, and forced her body to turn over. Fingers clutching onto a piece that might just be big enough to aid her, she used her free foot to kick at the beast. The tear into her leg was agonizing, and she cried out in pain. Adrenaline was the only thing keeping her from locking up. Swinging the rock madly, she lifted at her core and slammed it down onto the top of the wolf's muzzle. It made a noise, but it didn't let go.

It tugged and tugged. Her pants were tearing, and she was expecting it to rip her limb off at any second. Instead, what she felt was a dragging. Her clothing slipped up and her back and arms and sides obtained substantial wounds from being drug that fast across asphalt. It tugged and tugged at her. The speed it pulled her was alarming and eventually she lost her grip on the piece of parking lot she had been clinging to.

Crying out in pain, she was steadily kicking the wolf with the foot it didn't have in its mouth. The pain was unbearable and the more it dragged her, the worst it became. They passed the gas station and headed for the tree line. *No.* if it took her there, she was almost certain she wasn't going to make it out alive. She wished she'd had the thought to let Peter know she was coming, to tell someone when it might be a good time to worry about her. This was it? Jules had finally started to put her life back together; or was working on it at least. For nothing. To die in the forest dirt by a wolf.

Scrambling with the last of her energy, she couldn't grip anything. This wolf was fast. Strong. Her head bumped along until it connected hard with a fallen stump. The pressure caused her consciousness to fade. Her last thought: *it isn't even a full moon.*

What Julia hadn't expected was to wake up. The amplified ringing of her ears made her lift her hands to cover them. Her arm had pain shooting through it, making it hard to keep it raised. There was no way to readily identify where the pain was coming from. Everything hurt. As she tried to move, she felt her clothes stuck to her skin. The blood from her wounds had dried and the scabs were being tugged on when she moved in any direction.

Wherever she was, the floor was cold and covered in dirt. It was dark, but her eyes were adjusting a bit as she was able to make out that she was in some sort of cell. Julia was surprised by what she was seeing around her. It looked like something out of the medieval times. Forcing her body to stand, she was so angry she hadn't told anyone where she was going. Her friends at home would take a few days before realizing it was something to worry about. She and Peter were having an off time recently, so he wasn't expecting her to go missing.

"It won't matter." A voice Julia didn't recognize came from in front of her cell.

A tall, thin man came forward, his eyes glowing in the reflection of the dim lighting. There was zero doubt in Julia's mind that this was the wolf she had tried to fend off. He stood there, staring at her, without offering so much as an explanation. He was holding all the cards, so why would he try and explain anything?

"Why did you bring me here?" Julia asked, her eyes locked on his and her stance firm, though it hurt to stand at all.

The man simply moved around before dragging a scratchy metal chair from a corner and placing it in front of her cell. He tilted his head and smiled, his teeth too white and too sharp for her own comfort. "What's your name?"

Julia didn't answer, she grimaced as the pain in her body was starting to win over.

"Sit," he encouraged, clearing picking up on the shifting in her body language as she fought to stand strong.

Without a response, Julia stepped closer to the cell. Fear replaced with anger. "Why did you bring me here?" She asked him once more, this time through clenched teeth.

"Are you a witch, Julia?" He leaned forward, letting his hands fall freely between his knees. His thick black hair sliding forward and concealing the rest of his features in shadow.

"Not anymore," she said plainly. The pounding in her head was making her ears pop. Opening her mouth, she rotated her jaw to try to make it stop.

There was a long lasting silence between them. Julia had been through much worse than this. She had lost so much more than herself. This was nothing, even if she died. So rather than rattling off questions like a terrified, faded assembly of a final girl, she kept eye contact. She didn't move away. She stayed focused — at least as much as she could with her current pain level.

That seemed to amuse the stranger, as he smiled and said, "I like you." Julia's skin crawled with repulsion. "When I found you, or when *you* found *me* rather, I could tell something was different. I couldn't bring myself to devour you and leave your scraps for the vultures. So I drug you into the woods and brought you back here." He waved around the space as though giving her a tour of a grand entrance.

"I don't have any magic anymore. You're wasting your time. Kill me, or let me go."

The stranger wagged his finger at Julia before he stood up again. With his hands folded neatly behind his back, he paced. "That's not how magic works little duck. Your blood, your meat, it still contains that touch of light. Or in your case," his sinister grin grew unnaturally wide, "dark."

Swallowing what he said, Julia turned away from the cell and went to sit on the floor. What was his plan? Keep her there and bite her when he wanted a high? He was a wolf, not some sort of vampire. She was reeling over ideas, but without much strength (and certainly no magic), she had very few options.

Leaning her head back on the wall, she closed her eyes. All she could picture was Peter. Their first meeting in that hammock. The first time he met her friends. Their travels and adventures. His smile. His wavy hair. The way his eyes brightened up when he felt true joy. How caring and kind and funny he was. Julia's heart hurt just thinking about it.

"So what happened?" the stranger spoke, intruding on her thoughts as it finally dawned on her he could see them. "Your memories hurt to watch. Like a sad movie montage of unfortunate happy memories."

"There's nothing unfortunate about my memories." That wasn't always true, but it was when it came to Peter.

"Is it the darkness?" He was moving back to the chair now, sitting and staring at her. She hadn't opened her eyes yet, but she could feel it. "You're not going anywhere. What could hurt to indulge me?"

Opening her eyes up towards the ceiling, Julia rolled her head to the side and shook it slightly. "People argue. It is quite natural." She didn't owe him anything, but she would have to work extra hard to guard her thoughts.

"Right," the stranger said, nodding in a way that told her he wasn't buying it, "but what happened with you? I'm most curious."

"Please, just kill me already. Or do whatever it is that you want to do. I'm not playing these games with you and I am certainly not opening up to you." There was an odd laugh that came from the monster on the wrong side of the cage.

"Julia, my dear, I've been around for a really long time. I'm nothing if not patient. I get a little antsy sometimes, like when I go to get a few drinks and instead I rip out the throat of a convenience store worker. But I'm patient when I want to be."

Refusing to acknowledge anything he said, she simply looked at the floor. Once again, he was standing up, but this time he approached the cell. His hands slid down the bars and Julia watched, a bit unnerved at what he was contemplating.

"I'll make you a deal, witchy Julia. If you indulge me with your relationship problems, I'll give you something to ease the pain in the wounds I caused." His voice was so even and clear that it made Julia sick to her stomach.

"The least you could do..." Julia forced herself to stand, but she had to connect to the wall to keep herself upright. "Why do you care so much about my relationship? What is this to you?"

Wagging his finger at her just like before, he smirked. "Fair point. I'll answer you. I've lived down here for a long time, Julia. I've been alone most of that time. I don't come from some tragic story of love and loss. I've never loved anyone but myself. Perhaps that is why I'm like this. Honestly, it has been a life I prefer. But you definitely have something in your blood, and given your lack of surprise at what I am, I'm going to assume you know of wolves."

Julia took his quick pause as a chance to throw in her own thoughts. "I do recall running away and fearing for my life."

"Sure. Quickly followed by thoughts that I wasn't *your* wolf. Logic would lead me to the assumption that your lover, this Peter, is also of my kind."

Something hit Julia then. Her face grew hot and she found energy she didn't know she had. Slamming her hands down onto his that gripped the bars, she put her face up against the cell door almost touching noses. "Peter is nothing like *you*."

The stranger only grunted in reply to her attempt to hurt his hands. His eyes became a perfect golden ring and he snapped slightly changed canines at her. "Careful, darling. I bite."

Julia didn't back away or remove her hands. She maintained eye contact as she replied, "I've had worse." Letting her hands fall, she backed away and went back to her sitting position away from the bars.

"Yes, I've gathered," he said with a sneer she didn't care for. "What is your history exactly? You're not quite," there was a moment of pause as he eyed her curiously, "human. So what is it?"

Julia rotated her neck and shook off the frustration she felt, taking deep breaths. "Sorry to disappoint. But I assure you, that is all I am."

There was a way the rogue wolf nodded that made Julia uncomfortable. He knew more than he said. She wanted to ask how, but decided against it. "Well, I know that isn't true. And you should stop treating me like some incapable half-wit human from your circle of friends."

So, he didn't know everything. Her friends weren't what he would consider 'just humans' either. If he didn't know that, he had nothing. "Right. Then tell me what you know. I'm bleeding out and I'm growing tired of this game."

The man began to move around the room once more. Folding his arms over his chest, he never took his eyes off of her. Even when she didn't see it, she could feel it.

"It can be an interesting thing, when you attack someone. There's a certain level of energy that surges into your bloodstream. Especially if one is, say, high, or drunk. It can impact the way you feel when you're done feeding on them. An immediate rush. But something else can happen. If I were to accidentally attack another wolf, or fight one that I ended up biting, it can make me sick. It can make me want to vomit. Sometimes that feeling can last for days."

Julia closed her eyes for a moment and leaned her head back on the stone wall behind her. The longer this went on, the more exhausted she became. Her wounds were tingling, even though she had become used to some of it by now. Her head still ached and she was sure her stomach was in literal knots.

"You see, I have a sensitive palate. And when I bite someone who isn't human, I know." His eyes glowed again, pushing through the shadow that surrounded his face as he moved around the cave like prison. "And you, my pet, are not human."

Julia's throat constricted and she felt repulsed by this conversation. "I really wish you would just kill me. Listening to you talk about what you are, how you behave, is increasingly tedious."

He simply laughed. "Then perhaps you'll get your way and I'll bore you to death." He snapped his teeth at her through the bars. "It has been a long time since I've had anyone I could make listen to me. So you might as well get comfortable."

Julia shook her head. "How can you change like this? Without a moon?"

The man shrugged and tilted his head, intrigued she was finally engaging in conversation. "I'm different. It is that simple. And it is that complicated."

"So what? You were born a wolf? You committed some ultimate taboo and now you're cursed to change every night?"

"Oh no," he laughed, "I can change at will. Night, day, doesn't matter. And the reason is because I killed the person who started my bloodline. The short of that, very tiresome story, is that I didn't want to be a wolf. I didn't want to worry about life as a monster. So I killed the person who made me one. And then I didn't stop killing my own kind, until I reached the top of the completely made up food chain. When the originator of my, let's say clan to over simplify, died, I was gifted the ability to change at will."

Peter had never told Julia of a wolf like this. He'd mentioned rogues, which was an over generalization but she knew that. "Interesting."

There was an obnoxious sort of smirk on his features now, as Julia watched him carefully. "Well, then maybe you won't die of boredom." He shrugged. "I've spilled my guts, so to speak. What is your story? Why do you not taste like a human?"

The very question made her cringe and she looked away irritated. What difference did it make now? "I used to be more."

It was like the sight of Christmas in those worn eyes. He brightened up and drew closer to the side of the cell she was on. "I see."

"You probably don't. But the short of that, very tiresome story," she stopped to roll her eyes, "is that I used to be able to conjure magic, and now I can't."

Licking his lips, he made no effort to hide his enthusiasm. "So what? You were born a witch? You committed some ultimate taboo and then were stripped of your powers?" He was clearly proud of his own wit.

"I sacrificed those abilities for people I love. The source of my magic wasn't something I was born with. It had to be opened. It had to be taught. It was a gift. Truly." Julia took a moment to control the emotions that came forward as she talked about her inability to use magic anymore. "The only taste of it I've had since has been artificial."

The wolf before her almost did a jig at her words. "Ah yes, an addict. I knew it." He shook his finger at her. "Well, you are something else."

The word addict irritated her and she felt her nails digging into her skin to try to remain in control. "It is all gone now, and I don't use it anymore."

"It isn't," he said in just a tone above a whisper. "Whatever you had, it is still very much in your blood. Nothing is simply taught, fair Julia. These gifts of the world are not just thrown at you from a textbook or a written instruction. No, if you had it, you still have it. You're just in your own way."

Julia groaned and tried to stand but toppled over to her knees instead. "Just let me the fuck out of here!" she screamed. The anger consumed her, and she no longer cared how ridiculous she sounded or looked.

"I can't. I wish I could. But I can't. I need you." His voice lacked any emotions at all.

"Why? How?" Facing the ground, her hands were tangled in dirt as she wondered how this could have even come to pass.

"I'm not sure yet." She could tell those words were honest.

"Peter will eventually find me." Julia didn't know if that was even necessary. It was like lying to a stranger your mom was home, to pretend that would keep you safe.

"He will. You're right. He's close. He's strong." He smelled the air with his eyes closed and small smile. "I shall return when the time is right. I have a lot to think about."

With that he left the space and Julia crawled over to the gate. Banging and smacking the bars with her hands, she cried out to Peter to find her. If he *was* close, maybe her noise would bring him in. He'd know she wasn't safe and he wasn't the type to go blindly into any situation. This could be okay. Even if the rogue wanted Peter to come in, he'd be surprised to find that Peter was anything but a dumb animal.

"Jules?" Julia heard Peter's voice echo off the walls, but she couldn't quite tell how far away he was.

"Peter? I'm here! I'm here!" She started banging on the bars, but her efforts were not as loud as she had hoped.

There was a shuffling in the front of the entrance and she jerked her head up to watch. She wanted it to be Peter, but didn't want to call out again in case it wasn't. Her heart raced and her entire body felt full of electricity as her lover came into view. He shook his shaggy brown hair from his eyes as he locked gazes with her.

"Jules!" He rushed to the cell and gripped the bars as she mirrored his movement. Reaching through the bar, he could see her injuries and his eyes swelled with relief and fear.

"Peter, the guy who did this is here. He knows you're coming." Julia was choking on her emotions but she needed to warn him first and foremost. Her eyes fluttered shut as he touched her face through the rusted metal.

"I figured. I could smell him miles away. Your injuries..." he seemed to try and get a full look at her but she shook her head, "Right. We'll get there."

She wanted to say how sorry she was. She wanted to call out how fucked up she felt for all she had put him through. She wanted to profess how much she loved him and what he meant to her. It wasn't the time. They were in a predicament and all the energy she mustered at the sight of her partner was fading fast, reminding her how badly she was hurt.

Peter turned around to try and find a way into the cell, but he didn't waste a lot of time before he tried to rip the bars from the hinges. They were old, and after just a moment, he was able to pin the bottom of the door with his foot and yank it upwards to separate the metal. The door went limp and hung loosely as he let it fall.

There was a frozen moment in time where Peter embraced Julia. He touched her hair, her face. His nose went into her neck and brushed her cheek. This was the longest the two had been apart since they met, and it had been under very upsetting circumstances.

Peter turned from her and held her hands behind his back. "This isn't going to go how you think." He called out, but Julia didn't see the other man yet.

"You're probably right." He was coming into view, and he looked nothing short of amused, "I've never seen a wolf connect so willingly with a human. Maybe in the movies." He shrugged. "How do you want this to play out, pup?"

Peter let out a low growl. "There's only one way." Even though Peter couldn't change at will, he was incredibly strong. Julia wasn't sure what it meant against this monster of a wolf in front of them.

"I'm not going to fight you. I think I got what I needed." He smirked over Peter's shoulder towards Julia.

Peter tightened his grip briefly on Julia's hands and then stepped forward. Even Julia could feel the pressure in the air change. The other wolf stood still, eyeing Peter. This was dangerous. Julia didn't have any way to assist. She had no way to protect her lover or save herself. The longer she bled out, the weaker she felt.

The wolf in front of them let out a snort, and tilted his head to look at Julia. Peter was quick to move to block his line of sight. She had just experienced what it was capable of. Julia watched as the stranger lunged forward and right before her eyes he went from man to wolf. Everything seemed to be *absorbed* into the wolf version of himself.

She stood in shock as she watched the mouth of teeth clamp onto her lover's shoulders. Peter landed several hits, and was holding onto the beast when Julia noticed a jolt of energy in her arms. Glancing down, there was a golden electricity in her fingertips. The feeling of the magic she had lost was flowing through every fiber of her being. Closing her eyes, she sighed in ecstasy at the way it felt. Magic had always given Julia a high, and this was no different. Where was it coming from?

When Julia and Peter first met, there was an instant connection. Julia noticed when the two were in bed together, magic would return to her body for a few short (very specific) moments. Then it was gone again. He had ignited something within her and had told her more than once he was certain it was still inside of her. So had the stranger. All the traveling she had done to find magic, and she had never been any closer to reopening her body to her abilities.

The key, apparently, was Peter. As he fought with the wolf, she was pulled back to the moment when he yelped out in pain. The bigger wolf had him pinned and was biting him all over his arms. The warmth of the golden color pushed back up her fingers and Jules could feel it in her shoulders and her chest.

Extending her hands outward, she locked eyes on her target and then closed them. Visualizing him flying across the room and being pinned to the exterior wall on the opposite side of the cell, she kept her fingers pointed at him. The same tingling feeling grew in her fingertips and as she opened her eyes a gust of air removed the wolf from on top of Peter and pinned him to the wall. The snarling and growling grew louder.

"Jules?" Peter said, holding his chest and standing up. His legs had been scratched up as well, and he was a bit wobbly.

"I don't know." It was all she could say as she reached for him.

They were both in bad shape, but they needed to go before that hold wore off. Julia hadn't been able to do any magic of any kind for almost two years at this point, and she had no idea if she could do it again.

Wobbling through the exit, Peter helped Julia navigate the almost cave-like tunnel that led to the outside. There was a gaping wound on Peter's neck and shoulder from the wolf. Blood seeped all over his clothing and down his arm. Julia could feel it as she held onto him.

"I guess it is a good thing I'm already not human." He chuckled, Julia only stifled a smirk.

There was a slight breeze as they reached the edge of the entrance. Julia could see the sky, the trees, the ground. There was no vehicle and her car was still at the gas station. Wanting to put more distance between them, she knew their resources were limited.

"How far is—" Julia's words cut off by claws sinking into her shoulder and yanking her back.

Julia could hear Peter reacting but there was a fog in her mind as she tried to process the new pain, the old pain, and the situation. The massive wolf stood over her, drool and blood dripping onto her lower half. Julia kicked her feet into the dirt to move her body away. Her movements were substantially slower now that she had been bleeding and wounded for who knew how long.

The pain felt dulled for just a moment as she forced herself to stand. A snarl ripped through the air as the wolf had already turned his attention on Peter. Vision blurred, Julia knew once again she was weaponless. Forcing her hands outward, she tried to bring forward any magic left that she could muster; but her efforts remained futile.

Sounds of Peter's struggles filled the air, and Julia didn't care that she was without magic. She had to do something. Throwing herself at the wolf, she knocked her body hard against his in an effort to get him off of Peter. It worked, but only temporarily.

The wolf grabbed Julia by the throat and lifted her into the air, pinning her back against a tree. Restricting her airway, she flailed in his grasp as Peter lay motionless on the ground a few feet away. She had failed. This was all her fault.

If Julia had never abused magic, they wouldn't have had their time apart. She wouldn't have come to that gas station on her way in. She wouldn't have been snatched up by this wolf, and locked away. Peter wouldn't have had to come save her. None of this would have happened.

Reaching up, Julia copied the hold the wolf had on her, by gripping her fingers into his matted neck. Trying to focus on her grip, she wanted so badly to see that same golden glow as before. Instead, her grip grew tighter.

And tighter.

And then tighter still.

As her grip grew tighter, his weakened. Her airway was more clear and she gasped as she gripped harder still. Slowly her body lowered as the wolf was forced to let her go. The shock in his eyes was nothing compared to her own. Pushing into the grip, her body felt a new type of strength. Lifting her other hand, she did the same. Gripping and holding tightly as the wolf scratched at her arms and kicked at her to let go.

But she didn't.

She lifted the wolf in the air, a creature three times her size and weight. Slamming his back into the tree, she didn't let up. A low growl could be heard, but this time it wasn't from the rogue. It wasn't from her unconscious lover. It was from Julia.

Her hands wrapped as far around the beast's neck as she could and in one quick jerk of her wrists, she snapped his neck. The massive form slid into a motionless stupor at her feet. Blood coated her hands, and she realized her fingers had extended into sharp claws. They were already fading back to her normal hands.

Shaking, she backed away from the wolf and turned in time to see Peter trying to stand. Moving quickly to help him, she no longer felt the pains all over her body from her wounds. They were still there, she could feel the heat from them. They just weren't bothering her right now.

"Well," Peter coughed, leaning into her, "that's new."

Julia smirked down at him, completely unafraid of what this might mean. Julia had been around wolves and magic most of her adult life. What mattered right now was getting Peter help. In his human state, her wolf would have a hard time healing without assistance. Holding him around the hips, she started their trek back to her car.

"Do you think he did this on purpose?" Julia asked, not sure she could handle any sort of truth.

"I'm not sure. If he did, I don't think he intended on you killing him. But you remain, as always, full of surprises."

Julia gave the sound of a laugh, but it didn't reach her features. This wolf had been alone for all this time, and had gone out of his way to imprison Julia. She assumed, given their chat, that it was related to the magic within. So had he not meant for her to change? What were the rules of a bite from a wolf like that? Was it a combination of the supernatural already in her body with this wolf bite?

She hoisted Peter up a little higher in her hold, taking in mouthfuls of the outside air. That feeling of being trapped lingered. There had been a sense of certainty that had come over Julia, and she was certain she was going to die in that cell. And now? She was still alive with an added complexity. Peter had been able to bring out her magic before, but she had always assumed it was from the feelings he evoked. The way he made her feel as if she were capable of anything.

Maybe there was more to it.

Maybe this was how she got her magic back.

THE ETERNAL JUSTICE OF MAN

FIRE AND BRIMSTONE. A literal Hell on Earth. It had been prophesied since the beginning of time; the ultimate demise. Rot and ruin were all that remained of the once thriving planet. Those who had managed to save themselves were starving. Hardly anyone could live on the surface for more than a few days. The temperatures and barren wasteland drying out anything left of their mortal fluids. Everyone knew that attempting to prove this wrong was pointless, but humans can be oddly stubborn that way.

Far beneath the dirt and spoil, there was a makeshift lab. This lab sat in what used to be a military bunker. The bunkers were deemed inhabitable not long after the disaster that drove everyone underground. Militants were not there to aid the people who needed help. So long as they could save themselves and those they cared about, what were a few billion deaths for their cause? Nothing to bat an eye at, really.

In this makeshift lab, there is a man at work. Busying himself with tools, both power and medical. His hands are scarred from countless mishaps and his eyes are dull from years of disappointment. He adjusts his goggles one last time before he prepares to finish his cuts. There are men like this still. The good are not the survivors in stories of reality and truth. Evil simply prevails because evil will do what it takes. They do not care about the morality behind their decisions. They only care about their bottom line.

His name? This man of science who has (as they all do) decided to play God? He is simply known in the underground as *The Singularium*. No one knows his real name, and he doesn't know what others call him. He is the man who has stolen the stars. Encapsulating them into glass jars and pouring them into the bodies of the deceased. A beautiful account in some ways, but mostly he's just another mortal attempting to control that which he does not understand.

The Singularium has almost perfected his craft. Drawing inspiration from the constellations themselves, he is certain he is closing in on the perfect specimen. There are few who live in this underground place with him, but none of them are ignorant to the things he does. You can only go so long pretending not to smell the deterioration or to feel the rancid air, thick on your flesh.

Only a few days prior, a girl had gone missing. She wasn't sick, and she hadn't lost her way; so where was she? Anyone in their small circle could have guessed. Instead, they all pretended and made-up stories. It was far too easy to make the victim the villain than to stand up to the real problem.

"She must have gone to the surface," one had said.

"She never seemed right to me," another piped up..

"You're all liars." A voice came deep from the back of the line. Her mother's voice shot forward with grief. Yet, she had not lifted a finger to save her daughter.

Without interruption, he works. This time, he chose a killing method that would preserve most of her body. This one needs to look the part. She has to be beautiful and appear to have never been broken. He often looks at his projects as dolls, bringing them to life in a way no one else ever could. So many of them hadn't been dead to begin with.

The Singularium completes his procedure, save for adding life to the corpse. She looks beautiful. The perfect maiden. On the shelf behind his workbench, he retrieved the stars. Their name?

Virgo.

The virgin.

Purity incarnate.

"You look the part." His voice is barely above a whisper as he brushes back a few pieces of her blonde hair. Her eyes are sunken in slightly, and her cheeks are tight from the beginning stages of rigor mortis. He had stopped it just in time. There's no way to preserve a body down here. There are no options on the surface for such things either. At least beneath the surface, it remains cooler, albeit not the perfect conditions for working with dead bodies. Still, it's better than nothing.

Her skin is pale, and she looks so peaceful on the table. His eyes can not stray from her supple breasts and her perfectly untouched womanhood.

Clenching his teeth, the star killer has to refocus. Putting in the constellation is the hardest part of the process. It takes great energy and severe attention. And how? How had a mere mortal been able to capture something as mystical as a star? And not just one star, an entire constellation?

Before the world went dark, there was a man who wanted to be more than he was meant to be. Who dreamt of controlling the powers of the skies, and molding their magic in the palm of his hand for far more sinister things. Others wished for discovery, but this man wished for control.

This man built machine after machine. He was determined to touch the stars and pluck them from the safety of their sky. Many failed attempts finally resulted in a telescope that got him closer. He could almost taste the starlight on his tongue.

Then one day, he succeeded.

The mortal planned and meddled in an existence he would never be a part of. So, what happened when he touched their greatness? When he wrapped his sweaty palms around their magnificent extremities? The world fell into a cave of nothingness. Life and death were no longer opposites, but one in the same.

The man who controlled the stars had also single-handedly ended life as everyone on earth knew it. When he took his first constellation, the stars turned to dust between his fingers. A crimson powder that collected in a pile at his feet. Perhaps the dust would be usable in another fashion, but his efforts had not ended there. He wanted to harness these celestial beings. He wanted to use them to do his bidding and to create a world all his own. Earth had become merely a husk of what it was before. That gave him time to focus on his task: discovering a method of building something nightmarish with the stardust.

The Singularium has been building homunculus creatures for years. Stapling body parts and finding remains. What he had not anticipated was the ability for the stars to take on a life of their own. Not someone readily able to accept lack of control, he started learning to predict what might happen when a constellation was attached to a human form.

His first sign of progress was in using the constellation of Taurus. The woman was middle-aged, and more or less alone in the world. He had been too hasty. He was too eager. Cracking her skull wide open, he rushed to make his monster.

Her body twisted and changed into something else entirely after her stars were put in her body. Her human head splitting the rest of the way down, revealing the growth of a bullhead. The horns were what removed the last of the flesh from her scalp. He could *not* have predicted such a thing.

No matter how many times he tried to clean her up, there was always blood. Her fingers curled inward and began sticking together, much like that of a hoof. Her flesh hardened and sprouted little coarse hairs all over. This was not the flawless design he had hoped for. So, she went into a cage. Forgotten about and ignored.

Just like all the others who followed.

"You'll be different." His words are full of ill intent. His hands slide up her body and his fingers linger intentionally on her nipples. The maiden before him is his last real chance for success. He is losing time, and losing options.

Picking up the metal block used for tattooing, he prepares his needle. Grubby fingers grope at the blackened jar, spinning the lid, and lying it flat on his table. The dark red powder is added into a mixing container with black ink. This part of the process takes a lot of time. It is never good to rush this step, as it needs to be perfectly melded together. Too quickly and the powder will clump. A mistake he had made countless times already.

By the time the blending is complete, the dark liquid in the container has a brilliant red shimmer to it. The first time he saw it, he was mystified. He wanted to relish in the glory he had created. The first time he mixed these things, he was in awe of himself. How great of a man he must truly be to create something like this. There was no book to tell him how to do this. There was no legend passed on with hints on how to create star made vessels.

Now, it is just another tool on his table. All sense of magic and wonder had long since faded into the calloused skin of a bitter old man.

The humming of the machine comes on, and then off. Once more, on and then off. This happens a few times, frustrating the man-god in a way that makes him tap angrily at its sides. "Come on!" He growls.

Finally, the machine gurgles to a start, and stays on. He has to use as much of the ink as possible. Tattooing symbols on the body, he is never as creative with design choice as he is with his other goals. He covers her arms and legs with the symbol of her constellation. The ink and blood pool to the surface as he does his best to dab it away. This sort of blood is different.

The ink he dabs contains pieces of the star, so he is careful with his pressure. It's important to get as much into the skin as possible. This is the secret to his previous success. Even though his past "projects" have not been perfect, he still considers them necessary milestones. With greatness came sacrifice, and perfection was the cost.

But not today.

There was an attempt, many monsters ago, to drain the blood from the body to help with this process. The results were catastrophic. So now he leaves it. Tattooing dead flesh is no simple task. The elasticity is different, and the pores don't function the same. Still, he makes it work. Hours go by. Sweat and grime build on his forehead as he retains focus to finish.

The Singularium nears the emptying of the container, and he feels the body reacting to the presence of the star. It happened at different points depending on a lot of factors. That is why he has to do the last of it quickly. Line after line, he shades in the final symbol just as the liquid runs out. As he leans back into his chair, there is a loud popping sound from his bones. He is exhausted. Completing the task, his breathing becomes a bit strained as he looks up and sees his maiden's eyes open. They are solid white, like marble. There is no pupil. There is no color.

Her skin seems to pulse, a bright red vibration. The outline of her markings shimmers with her coagulated blood. Chunks fall onto the floor as she sits up and attempts to move from the table. Gripping the sides of it, the man watches her in awe. She is perfect. Beautiful. His hands are outreached, and there is a smile broad across his features.

The muscles are so tense.

A smile is so foreign.

It hurts.

Virgo stands in the feeling of her agony. Every part of her being is on fire. The magic burns a hole through any final shred of humanity she has left. Her milky gaze takes in the man in front of her. A longing she doesn't recognize rises in her chest. *Sadness?* She feels pain and sadness. *Why?* There is nothing there to explain the feelings. There is nothing inside to remind her of who she was. To tell her who she had been. Her memories are like faded pictures in a flip book.

Attempting to get her bearings in the room, some things she remembers quite easily. Motor functions are almost completely normal, as the constellation has no issue moving off the table and closer to the stranger before her. The man, her presumed captor, is in a stupor beside her. He sits as though waiting for some sort of praise for what he has created. Bloodied fingers trace lines over the tools she finds on his table. Her back to the stranger now, she feels her way around the metal in front of her. Virgo is aware of the man as he stands up and approaches her. His hands grow closer to her shoulders. Her naked form is crusted in ink and lumps of rotten blood.

Strands of her yellow hair cling to her, drenched in rust-colored plasma. She doesn't feel any hesitation as her fingers grip the handle of a hammer. Just as his fingers pressed into her crumbling flesh, she turns in one swift motion, landing the hammer on the side of his head. The force of the hit leaves a hole above his ear. One eye slumps downward, and the other is wide in shock.

The Singularium does not speak, but his mouth falls agape as if he wants to say something. What would he say to her? Traitor. She feels the look of betrayal in his eye as he falls into her.

"Disgusting," she hisses, stepping back and letting him fall. The hammer remains in her hand, and she knows she isn't finished.

Loud noises erupt from the metal walls as the hammer clatters to the floor. She puts her hands over her ears, as the sounds of her sisters grow too loud.

"Be still," she whispers, the voice even and strong. The noises settle for the time being and she is able to finish what she started.

Taking a pair of pliers, she leans over the man. In his aura, she feels his responsibility for the damnation of the stars. All his greed and selfishness surface like ink on a page. Pain courses over her thoughts, and she can now feel all of the wreckage and pain he has created. She knows who this was, and she understands the role he played in the pain she's felt. The pain they all felt.

He is still breathing for the moment, but the trauma to his head will claim his life soon enough. Wanting him to feel but a fraction of her own discomfort, she snips each of his fingers from both hands. He wiggles a bit in her grasp, but he had already made the mistake of thinking he was stronger.

"As all men do," she whispers down at him, not ashamed to admit to herself it feels good to watch him squirm.

Standing up, she looks around the room for a moment longer before her attention lands on something that she knows she can fashion around her head. Barbed wire cut her palms as she shapes it into a crown. Extending the metal, she forces his removed fingers down onto the makeshift posts. Smaller fingers on the outside, leading toward the center with his two middle fingers. Bending them in, she stacks her crown upon her head.

These were the fingers of a monster. There were the fingers of a thief. A rapist. A kidnapper. A human man who thought he could be a god. Her lips curve into a crooked smile, blood sliding down the sides of her face from the crown, pushing into her crest. The surrounding noise erupts again. "I'm coming, my loves."

Virgo steps over the man's body and does not give him the satisfaction of a final look. The room is dark away from the table, but she does not need the light. Her vision seems to be obscured in her new condition. What she can see is glowing. The blue aura is almost like an echo of the things occupying the space around her.

The cages are lined in rows on both sides of a small hallway. There are twelve cages, but only a few conceal her siblings. Others are open and left uncovered. *Humanity doesn't deserve us.* The anger grows inside of her the longer she is conscious.

If there had been anything left of a heart, it would have been broken. Even in their calmer state, her siblings' pain and suffering is fresh in the wounds of the maiden. Her ears are ringing with their silence, and slowly the memories from before flood her mind. This man who deemed himself worthy. All the victims he created, including the stars themselves. What of the ones who *let* him do this? The people who held the same level of accountability for his heinous acts. The man had clearly never fathomed he'd be outdone by a creation. He became too confident, and his arrogance was his downfall. No, Virgo would not find herself in a cage.

Shredded tarps drape over each metal prison. Her siblings are eager to see her and feel free once again. Yanking the tarps away individually, she can hardly believe what she finds: shredded skin patched up around the face of a bull. Blood and brain matter all over the floor, collecting in a pile of sludge. She is hunched over and can barely fit. Her hoofed fingers and toes could barely keep her up in the tiny space. A snort of recognition, and Virgo reaches in her fingers to touch her nose. She caresses it slowly before yanking at the lock, tearing it and the door from the hinge.

As Virgo watches her sister get acclimated to standing once more, she moves on to the other cages. One holds a figure with oval black eyes, her mouth open wide with razor-sharp teeth. As she examines closer, Virgo pulls open the door and watches as a crimson skinned beauty comes forward. Her hands extend in claw like fashion, and the fabric on her torso is shredded for the tiny legs that came from her ribs.

The next several cages are empty, but a whimper of longing escapes the next one covered in tarp. She wonders if he covered them to hide the shame of what he had done, or the disgust he felt for his abominations. For that is all they were to him. Mistakes he'd had to learn from.

The whimpering grows silent as Virgo pulls down the tarp and bends over to tug the lock away, allowing her sister space to come out. Even in the dim room, she can see the noise is coming from an extended snout. Two beautifully carved horns curl into almost bun-like masses on top of her stretched head. There is a tuft of hair that extends past her chin and as she crawls forward, Virgo catches sight of her stunningly white tail.

They all stand together in a row, each staring at one another with love and admiration. "Enough," Virgo says.

The simple word is all that is needed to tell them exactly what she means. Even with this man dead, the evil is not over. How many people knew what he was doing and let it happen? How many times had they watched and remained silent? *Enough.*

Sounds of metal and shuffling echo off the walls around them as the constellations take up anything that could be used to hurt the outsiders. Virgo carefully wraps and places the remaining stardust jars into a bag at her side. She can't stomach leaving them behind.

With her crown of fingers, and her blood covered form, she doesn't hide the shame of this new body. She remains nude, bloodied, and inked. A reminder of what this monster had done, and what she has overcome.

Her fingers move quickly to undo the locks upon the large metal door and it creaks open loudly with an alarm of death. Turning back over her shoulder, she looks at each of her sisters. "Leave no one alive." Her words spew with the venom she has for these people. First things first, she is going to find the one her host called *mother.*

Throughout the tunnels, the sound of chaos erupt. Screams and the shrieks of power tools. Each life that is taken gives them strength to take another. The noise must have reached the small room where this mother woman lived. She is cowering in a corner when Virgo finds her. Her eyes are wide and tears spill down her cheeks. There is a moment of relief when she sees it is her daughter. Only, it isn't.

Blade in hand, Virgo shoves the knife into the woman's abdomen and twists. The sounds she makes soothe the constellation. "You're not worthy of being a mother. And so," Virgo tilts her head, "you'll be nothing."

Gripping the blade handle, she digs it deeper and yanks it up. The handle snaps halfway up the woman's form, but that doesn't stop the maiden. Sliding her hand down, she holds the raw blade and, making sawing motions with her arm, she continues cutting up the woman clinging to life. She doesn't scream, she only sobs.. Her pain physically is nothing compared to the pain her daughter felt. That is something Virgo needs to make sure she understands.

A planner by nature, the constellation had a goal from the moment of her re-birth. Take the lives of those who watched, and kill the one they called The Singularium. The destroyer of worlds. Once this is done, they shall know true freedom. Whatever they find in the outside world, they'll take it on with a new strength and insight.

Once the woman stops moving, the maiden looks down at her bloodied legs. On the floor around her feet and ankles rest various pieces of the woman's insides. It feels warm and soft. The wet texture sends a thrill down Virgo's spine. Dropping the knife, she tilts her head and lets the body crumple to the floor into a forgotten mass.

"Nothing," she whispers down to the corpse. The smile on her face is one of gratitude from the girl's body she now claimed as her own.

Exiting the room, she can see Taurus. She holds a young man by his arm, ramming her horns into his chest. Virgo is proud of her sister, and she doesn't look away until the bloodied chest cavity is parted and there is no life left in his eyes. With a nod of respect to her sibling, she moves down the dirt path of the running humans.

There are more than she realized, but it will make no difference. Where could they go? What could they do? A sharp pain in her belly causes the maiden to look down. As she does, she sees her dead insides trying to escape the hole in her body. Looking up, she sees a girl with a gun. Her face is terrified and her hands are shaking.

In two easy strides, the maiden is able to grip the girl's wrist and snap it back, bone protruding just beneath her palm. "We are born of stars and magic. You can do nothing but watch us and worship us."

Wrapping the girl's arm backwards, she uses it with great force to snap her neck. She was too young. Too young to know the pain of the world she existed in. Yet, old enough to die. No one is truly virtuous.

"My fair Cancer," Virgo coos at her sibling as she uses her pincers to cut pieces of flesh from her current victim. Hunks of bloodied tissue, and skin fall in heaps around her, as their blood sprays across her jagged smile.

As the maiden continues walking, she looks for their other sibling, wondering who she had found to exact her vengeance on. Aries is down on all fours. She is clomping her hoofed hands and feet down, trampling the bodies of someone, or multiples, to a barely unrecognizable mess. Human matter of all sorts clings to Aries' hooves and her legs. Her face reflects nothing but peace and retribution.

The screams quiet down and the life force that had once belonged to the undeserving now nestles into the bosoms of the constellations. They all stop in the same stride to turn back and look at their destruction. The world has fallen to ruin and so have all the people left that inhabited it. It is time for a change.

The poorly lit path leads to a metal railing and a large silver room, leaving behind all the buckling homes and dismantled bodies in collapse. Virgo stands before her sisters, confident. She is ready to face the outside world with them at her side.

"When we go out here, we fix the world to our liking. We've been left and forgotten for too long. Women on this earth are not high in number, but they are even less in value. We must change that. What are the stars if not beacons of hope for those who gaze upon us?"

Her sisters nod in agreement; their bloodied bodies standing strong and at the ready. Their pain and suffering will not be in vain. They will have their day in the sun and the reckoning will follow. The Singularium had been wrong to assume he could control such power, but perhaps he was right to destroy the world for all it had become.

Pushing open the large metal door to the surface, Virgo steps out into the heat of the decaying world. Her feet slide against the hot sand. The heat is a sensation she welcomes. Looking out at the lifeless existence before her, she smiles.

"Stars are not meant to be kept in jars by men who seek to defile them."

All at once, her sisters stand behind her. They, too, mirror the smile of the maiden.

ADDITIONAL CREDITS

- "Soul Eater" was previously published in *Something Bad Happened*, edited by Jennifer Bernardini

- "The Eternal Justice of Man" was previously published in *Horroroscope Vol 1*, edited by Harriet Everend

Both stories were edited down and altered quite a bit for these anthologies. I went back through both stories and put back in things I had removed and had them re-edited for a new fresh take on two of my favorite stories.

Cover design services for the beautifully creepy. Premades, customs, magazine covers, etc.

Twitter: @grimpoppydesign

Patreon: patreon.com/grimpoppydesign

About the Author

Angel Krause is a horror content creator under the YouTube channel Voices From the Mausoleum. From movies, to video games, special fx, and more, Voices covers anything under the horror umbrella. Angel has stories in a few anthologies but All The Little Voices is her first published work of her own. You can find Angel on all social media platforms under Voices From the Mausoleum.

Other Collections Under Voices:

Livestock: Stories From the Un-Herd
That Old House: The Bathroom
That Old House: The Bathroom Part 2

Printed in Great Britain
by Amazon